Levity

A Gay Fairy Tale

Leta Blake

Prologue

ONCE UPON A time, there was a kingdom at the edge of what was and what could never be. At the center of this kingdom was a castle, and within this castle was a king. Inside this king was a terribly selfish heart.

One summer day, as the river ran, the birds flew and the flowers bloomed, King Leo paced by his queen's chamber door, listening as she labored. After three bastard daughters and one bastard son, King Leo was impatient for his queen to present him with an heir to the crown.

He banged a fist against the door, raging

at her to hurry, so that he might hold the babe aloft for the gathered crowds to see. "And God help you if it isn't the son I deserve."

But the birth was hard going.

Finally, he heard the midwife shout, "I see the head, my queen."

The king flung open the door, strode into the room and pushed aside the old crone attending to his wife. His wife lay back against the pillows, golden hair spilling around her, and her grey as dust. She rested quietly in a damp circle of sweat and blood.

Her pale face shone from prior effort, but still he cursed her laziness. "Push, or find out what it is to defy me!"

She struggled up to her elbows to obey. As the queen gave another great cry, the child burst forth into the king's waiting palms.

He gripped the small body under its armpits and raised it up. There, before his eager eyes, dangled the child's penis. The king turned away from his sobbing wife, ignoring her outstretched hands and whimpers for her son.

He strode across the room and flung open the shutters to lean out of the queen's high tower chambers. His hands gripped the baby's body firmly as he thrust it into the light of the day. He yelled, "Kneel before your prince! Kneel before my son!"

The sun illuminated the wailing infant until he appeared to fairly glow, and the gathered crowd let out a wild cheer, collapsing to their knees.

As the news of the child spread, joy cascaded through the kingdom. Perhaps this prince would be good and handsome and wise. Perhaps he would be different from his father. And, as with every birth across endless time, hope was reborn.

Chapter One

"IT'S MY BIRTHDAY," Efrosin sang, bobbing in the air near the ceiling of his bedroom, as was his wont. He was wearing his usual silk pajamas, and Geoffry felt a prick of concern regarding his chances of convincing his charge to change into more appropriate finery.

"Indeed it is, Your Highness. Many happy returns to you," Geoffry said.

Efrosin pushed off the stone wall with his bare feet and skimmed through the air. "As my manservant, Geoffry, it is your duty to help me get what I want."

His short golden hair was still wet and

disheveled from his usual morning routine—several hours spent swimming in the embrace of the river. Geoffry imagined that if it were not for the traditional wreath-laying ceremony upon the late queen's grave, Efrosin would soon be ready to leave to further frolic in the depths and shallows of the river.

Not that Geoffry could blame his charge for his obsessive love of water. Due to the misfortune of having been cursed soundly by a vengeful witch when he was but an infant, in the water was the only place where Efrosin had any weight at all.

Obviously feeling anything but unfortunate, Efrosin spun about mid-air without a care in the world. Geoffry turned from him and began to set out the proper outfit—including a specially designed coat with many long, colorful ribbons sewn firmly to the hem. Each ribbon would be held by a knight to prevent Efrosin from floating into the great, blue sky. Geoffry straightened the collar on the coat and pondered how best to persuade Efrosin to put it on.

"I hope that what you want, sire, is an afternoon ceremony beside your mother's grave," Geoffry said. "For that is what you shall have. Come now, we should hurry. There isn't much time."

Efrosin pushed off the ceiling and took the white, silver and gold embroidered shirt from Geoffry's hand. "If I must do something quite so dull, then you must entertain me with one of your fine tales first, Geoffry."

"Put on these clothes, sire, and I'll consent. What tale would you like to hear?"

"The one of my birth would be rather appropriate, don't you agree?"

"You know that one by heart, sire. I've no doubt you could tell it yourself quite well enough."

But Geoffry knew it wasn't true. Due to his cursed condition, Efrosin lacked emotional gravity and could never pitch his voice to the right note sof grief, having never felt anything close to the emotion himself. Geoffry had often noted that Efrosin, in his unwitting callousness, best liked tales that evoked great sadness in others. He clearly found their unhappiness fascinating and even amusing.

Pulling the shirt over his head, and taking the pants Geoffry offered, Efrosin took Geoffry up on his suggestion. "Once upon a time, a beautiful queen—my mother—gave birth to a handsome and blessed son." Efrosin frowned. "Hmm, maybe if I skip to the good part?" He cleared his throat and tried again, "Sadly, she was overcome with fever and never recovered from childbed. The country went into great mourning over the loss of her grace and kindness. The kingdom truly suffered when she died."

Efrosin dove down through the air to grab hold of Geoffry, and, with his help, put on the heavy, beribboned coat. "It's much better when you tell it," Efrosin said, a haze of dissatisfaction almost clouding his face before evaporating. "It's my birthday," he repeated, and this time there was a note of determination that set off a warning bell in Geoffry. "And, as I was saying, a prince should have what he desires on his birthday."

"Yes, your eighteenth," Geoffry said warily. "You're a man now, sire." Geoffry hoped, even though he knew it was useless, that by saying it aloud Efrosin might feel even a small portion of the burden associated with his upcoming responsibilities as Crown Prince. "And as for what you desire, well, you should take that up with your father."

The king had decided the time had come to make a strong alliance with one of several neighboring kingdoms, in order to strengthen his position for another war. To that end, Geoffry knew the king intended as his birthday gift to present his son with a selection of several princesses and princes— one of whom was to become Efrosin's spouse.

Being fair of face and having grown into

the lean, strong body of a man, Efrosin should have been an ideal husband. Yet because of his cursed condition, his temperament and urges were still very much those of a boy. And, understanding Efrosin better than anyone, Geoffry knew the marriage would be doomed to misery and unhappiness for whomever was chosen.

"Truly, I would rather not go. It's so terribly boring."

Geoffry said, "It is important that your people see how much you honor the woman who died giving life to you."

Efrosin seemed to ponder this. "Well, I am very happy to be alive. It would be awfully dreary to be dead."

"Yes, quite. Now come, let me call Sir Carlisle and the others."

Geoffry was greatly relieved when Efrosin consented. He watched Efrosin closely during the ceremony, though, and noted that beneath Efrosin's expression of cheerful boredom, there was an unmistakable glimmer of excitement. A hard knot grew in Geoffry's stomach. The king, who could barely be bothered to look anything but bored himself, didn't seem to notice. But then, that was nothing new.

BACK IN EFROSIN'S room, the sun glowed bright in the early afternoon sky, and Geoffry's fingers shook as he undid the buttons of Efrosin's coat while Efrosin bobbed low to the ground where the knights held him fast with the ribbons.

As soon as the coat was off and the knights dismissed, Efrosin's smile grew so big that Geoffry felt his middle-aged heart might fail him. It was never a good sign when Efrosin looked quite that delighted.

"I am no longer a child, you realize," Efrosin began. "And you must follow my orders. You will tie a rope to my ankle—this one here, the right one, because the left is much too pretty for rope burn, you see—and fly me like a kite, high, high above the tallest tree. So, it must be quite a long rope."

Geoffry's mouth went dry. His eyes went to his time piece and he noted the king would be having his afternoon nap. The punishment for waking him was death or dismemberment, or sometimes both. He cleared his throat.

"Indeed, sire, and while I'm sure it would be a great adventure for you, it would be terrifying for me. What if I were to stumble, drop the rope, and you were to blow away? It isn't as though you're a balloon. We couldn't simply have a good marksman on hand to shoot you down again." He set about needlessly polishing the prince's shoes. How could they be scuffed when they never touched the ground? "And I'm equally sure that we do not have a rope of such a length." This, surely, would be enough to dissuade the young daredevil.

The prince may not have understood the gravity of the proposal, but Geoffry certainly did. He would never forget the violent lashing he'd received when Efrosin was but twelve and had managed to make a rope from lengths of sheets and float himself out the window while Geoffry slept. Though the boy claimed it was an unplanned, impulsive adventure, Geoffry had seen the glint of mischief and glee in the child's face as he'd read the bedtime story that night, and he'd suspected that Efrosin might take his closed eyes as an invitation to adventure.

But could Geoffry be blamed for falling asleep despite his best efforts? He was no longer such a young man, with his dark hair graying at the temples and aches in his bones when he did not rest. Besides, who impulsively tied together ten lengths of bed sheets? At some point, one must begin to recognize what one is doing and it then becomes a plan.

"As it happens," Efrosin said, pushing his foot against the ceiling to propel himself downward and drifting weightlessly toward the tall post at the foot end of the bed, "I have requisitioned such a one from the ropemaker. I summoned him last week while you were at market. Surprise! Now you have no excuse."

Geoffry wished to call his prince a scamp and beat his tail with a birch rod, as he would his own child for such foolishness, but he knew it would do no good. He remembered well a day during Efrosin's tenth year when the king decided to forcibly instill some gravity in his free-floating son, declaring that boy would indeed be sobered by the time he was done.

The screams of pained laughter Efrosin had let out as his father had beat him still haunted Geoffry's worst nightmares. At times, sweating from dreams of it, he wished he had interceded—his own beating be damned—for he had known it would change nothing.

And it had not. The king had left Efrosin's chambers with a rare look of humiliated defeat, abandoning Efrosin naked on his stomach, with his back, buttocks and thighs striped from the switch, and delirious, broken laughter drifting from his smiling mouth.

Geoffry's own eyes had filled with tears when Efrosin had giggled, "That rather hurt a lot, Geoffry. I do so wish that I could cry. Tell me, would that make it feel better?"

"No," Geoffry had said. "It would not." Though, he'd thought, perhaps it would.

"Oh, well then, if only I could cry then at least Father would not be so cross." Then he'd laughed some more. "Usually, he is so funny when he is cross."

But something told Geoffry that, despite Efrosin's laughter, he did not find his father so very funny at that moment. It had been a difficult night for Geoffry, applying salve to his princeling's wounds and crying tears in Efrosin's stead. The king had never tried such a thing again, and now seemed resigned to his son's flighty ways.

"You requisitioned a rope so that I may fly you as a kite," Geoffry repeated slowly.

"Indeed. And it shall be jolly and grand. Just think, Geoffry, I'll see the top of the castle. I'll see where the river flows. Perhaps I'll even see—"

"You saw the top of the castle the time you broke free of your handler and floated up to the top of the highest turret. And poor Michaelson nearly fell and died trying to fetch you down."

Efrosin's lips curved up into a wide smile. "Oh yes, that was a brilliant day. But that was not quite the same. That was a mistake, you see, and I was a bit frightened, which made it an ever so sharp joy to float that high. This will be more sedate, and you are always imploring me to be sedate."

"Sire…"

"Come," Efrosin called, gripping the poster of the bed firmly and shoving himself toward the door with the effortless grace of a balloon drifting through the air. "Let us begin."

Geoffry's heart sank. There was nothing to be done for it. He hoped it didn't hurt too badly when he was hanged. And that would be a just punishment if he got caught holding onto the end of Efrosin's rope while the boy floated in the heavens. If Efrosin should float away…well, there was no telling what would happen to Geoffry, or his wife and five children.

Geoffry crossed himself and followed Efrosin as he slowly bounced through the hallway, his feet always at least three feet above the ground.

EFROSIN HAD NEVER been so high before. Well, not on purpose. Well, not lately. And then he was even higher. He gazed down at dear Geoffry, who looked so tiny on the ground, both hands clenched around the end of the rope as though it took effort to keep Efrosin from floating away, when he was as light as air itself.

He could see the preparations for his birthday feast being made on the other side of the line of trees separating the field from the castle garden. He laughed as he imagined the great fright the servants would have if they would but look up and see him there in the sky like an angel of the ether.

"I should have Geoffry construct wings," he declared, his eyes shining at the thought.

He felt a stab of high-spirited annoyance that he had not thought of it before. "It would have been the most divine entrance to my party."

If he'd had it in him to mourn that this idea had come to him much too late, he'd have mourned. As it was, he turned to count the clouds, and called down to Geoffry the many wonders of their beauty. Then he spent a few minutes casting about for a sound other than the whistling of wind in his ears, which was so much sharper than the burble and rush of water.

"Lo, but it is lonely up here," he said at last, his eyes following the green of the fields cutting a swath down to the path taken by the blue river.

Geoffry had argued admirably that Efrosin celebrate his birthday with another swim instead of a flight, and Efrosin had been tempted. The river, much more than the air, was his best friend. It alone held him in a snug and secure embrace, with just the right amount of gravity to prevent him from floating away.

He'd spent much of his life in the water, bobbing in his own world, splashing and laughing, and sunning for endless summer days. The river calmed him, and was the only place he could be persuaded to listen long enough to have learned his letters and numbers. Efrosin remembered his tutor in a boat, umbrella held over his bald head, teaching Efrosin to conjugate verbs as he swam in circles or floated dreamily on his back, his ears below the water, and the professor's rumbling words lost in the tumble of the current.

In comparison, the air was an ocean of risk, at once compelling and terrifying. It was godless, empty, full of distance and height, and Efrosin could vanish into it entirely, never to be seen again.

He sometimes dreamed he'd floated as high as the constellations and the endless, cold horror of it would startle him, laughing, from his sleep. "Oh what a wondrous thing," he'd exclaim, his blood coursing in his veins. "What a terrible thrill."

And yet he was drawn to it like a moth to a flame.

He'd never told anyone—not even Geoffry—that it frightened him so, and that perhaps it wouldn't be quite so very bad to have his gravity returned to him. He'd been told he was born with it, but couldn't remember ever possessing an ounce of substance.

As fate would have it, Efrosin had no sooner decided that he'd had enough of the thin air for the day and that a swim would, indeed, be a better way to pass the time until his birthday celebration, than a black-winged bird flew past his face. It reared around and beat its wings like cupped hands scooping the air to pause mid-flight before him, and screeched.

The bird seemed to smile, something eerie and white, as red flashed in its eyes. Then it dove for the rope tied securely around Efrosin's ankle, landed on it like a sideways clothes line, and tore into the rugged material with a razor-sharp beak.

"Stop! Whyever are you doing that?" Efrosin asked, a giddy burst of fear shaking him, and he started to laugh hysterically. "I shall float away if you break the rope."

Panicked, he looked down toward Geoffry, who had noticed the bird's quick work at severing the prince from his tenuous link to the earth. Efrosin descended through the air rapidly in quick, desperate jerks as Geoffry attempted to reel him in before the damage was done.

"Shoo!" Geoffry screamed. "Sire, kick him away."

Efrosin tried, he truly did, but could not move downward through the air that wished to suck him up into its deadly embrace. Then in one dizzy moment he felt it—the moment the rope broke, and he flew free.

The wind made off with him, rushing him away from the field where Geoffry stood with the long rope coming down on his head, yelling helplessly for Efrosin. Efrosin was pierced with agonizing exhilaration. His destiny was at hand. He could feel it. The sky that had been his nightmare and fascination since youth would bear him away to his end.

The clouds whispered across his face, and he laughed in mad, spasmodic hiccups until it became quite hard to breathe. It was all so very funny. The Light Prince met his end as an escaped human kite, the people would say.

Efrosin could not stop his wild laughter.

DMITRI WALKED THE familiar path through the woods to check the traps again. It had been a full week since he'd caught anything, though he wasn't concerned. Fishing had been plentiful, and he looked forward to harvesting fresh berries and vegetables from his garden later in the month. Still, he did need meat to cure and put aside for winter.

There was only himself to provide for, but he never knew when there might be another drought, as there had been the year Queen Inna died. He had no memory of it himself, having been just a toddler at the time, but his father had told him often of the hunger that gripped the people and animals, and of the scarcity that had ended many lives. It was one of the more exciting stories in Dmitri's father's repertoire, and he'd asked to hear the tale often as a boy.

There were many important lessons in the stories Dmitri's father told, of course, but one of the most important had been to think well in advance on matters of survival. So Dmitri did just that, always putting away more than enough meat to weather any famine or provide for an unexpected visitor. Not that a visitor happened by very often. Yet when one did, Dmitri wanted to make a good impression, in case they could be prevailed upon to stay longer, or, at the very least, return for a visit.

As he rounded the bend that would take him to the boundary, a limit he could sense from several yards in advance, he happened to look up. As he did, his mouth fell open and he dropped his sack.

There, tangled in the tree limbs above him, was an angel. It had to be an angel because his face was inhumanly beautiful with rosy cheeks and lips, and his hair was such a color that it was surely made of gold itself. His white garments were covered with fine silver detail that glittered in the sunlight. He hung there as though weightless, defying the earth's pull, actually tugging the branches up, instead of causing them to droop with the burden of holding him.

Dmitri fell to his knees, and as he stared, the angel's eyes opened, taking him in. A tremulous laugh reached him, and Dmitri blinked in confusion.

"Blessed be the west wind," the angel called out. "Or I should have surely been lost forever. And that would have been entirely unfortunate, because it's my birthday, you see, and no one should be lost forever on their birthday."

Dmitri shook his head, trying to clear the strange vision. Had he fallen asleep in the cabin and dreamed of checking the traps? Was he dreaming still? What an odd thing for an angel to say. Dmitri had never given thought to whether or not angels had birthdays. He supposed they very well might.

"So—you will fetch me down, of course."

"But how will you go back up?" Dmitri asked, noticing now the angel's distinct lack of wings. Had he been injured and lost them in the fall? Or had they been removed? Was he a bad sort? Tossed from heaven like Lucifer? Would God expel an angel on his birthday? If so, he must have done something especially wicked.

"Go back up." The angel chuckled. "Well, that would be easy enough if I wanted to go up, but I assure you that I've had quite enough of up to last forever." The angel shook with mirth again. "Or until tomorrow. Or whenever I'm overcome with the lust for it once more. It's quite delightful, except that it's terrifying. Which is, of course, how so many of the best things are."

Was that any way to speak of heaven? Dmitri tilted his head; he took in the angel's bare feet and the short rope tied to one ankle. "Are you an angel?" he said, deciding it was best to get that part out of the way at once.

"No. I'm a prince. Surely you've heard of me? The Light Prince. Efrosin? Son of Leo, King of Goldenthal? We're truly quite famous in these parts, given that it's our kingdom." The peals of laughter should have been insulting, but seemed without malice to Dmitri's ears.

Of course he'd heard of the Light Prince. But he'd thought the tales told by the old crones and beggars passing through were exaggerated, as most tales are. Yet the man hung there before Dmitri in a tree, as though he were a kite, still being tugged by the breeze.

"Truly, it is life or death," the Light Prince said. "I know it must not seem very serious given my disposition and inability to stop laughing—because it is incredibly funny—but I assure you that I cannot help that, and should you leave me here much longer, the wind will have its way and I'll be cast upon the mercy of the heavens again."

Dmitri took in his blinding smile and tried to reconcile the chipper tone of voice with the professed circumstances. Hadn't the travelers who'd told him stories of the Light Prince said that the malady extended to his manner and personality, resulting in a perpetual lack of depth to any grave feeling?

"If it's a hope for reward money that has you dallying about, let me assure—"

"No! Of course not. Certainly I'll help you, my good prince, but I must admit I've never fished a weightless man from a tree before. How do I start, sire?"

"Start by calling me Efrosin, or I will laugh myself into a stupor with your 'good prince' here and 'sire' there, and general attitude of obeisance. I am not my father, and it will only make me piss myself with giggles to have you bend and jump at my every breath. So I beg of you to take pity, and not make me laugh any harder than I already am."

"Yes, my…Efrosin."

"Quite right. Now, your Efrosin believes that Geoffry usually fetches a rope—truly, he always has one handy since I must be tied down so very often. Then he climbs the tree, ties the rope to my wrist or ankle before also tying it to his own, lest he lose his grip on me. The rest I'll tell you when we are face-to-face."

He sounded coy and Dmitri wondered at that but only long enough for Efrosin to burst into gales of laughter. "You should have seen your expression," he cried. "So shocked! So very funny!" And as his body shook, the branches seemed to loosen their grip on Efrosin's body. There was no time to waste.

Dmitri grabbed his sack, ripped the cord from the drawstring closure and started up the tree. He scaled it as quickly as possible, glad the boundary only applied to the land and that the sky had no power to confine him. As he reached the limbs beneath the prince, he grabbed hold of Efrosin's ankle, the one with a length of rope still dangling from it, and tied the rope to his own ankle.

When it was fastened, he quickly bound Efrosin's wrist to his own with the cord and worked to unhook the prince's silky clothes from the twigs and small branches. Then he grabbed Efrosin's outstretched hand, jerked, and was shocked when the man flew without any resistance toward him, weighing less than a puff of cotton.

As their bodies collided, Dmitri gripped Efrosin around the waist, and he stared into Efrosin's handsome face. Endless laughter filled Efrosin's blue eyes, and his lush mouth was shiny with an abused look about his open lips, as though he'd been biting them in an unsuccessful attempt to stop his mirth. Dmitri had never seen a human being so beautiful.

Dmitri didn't understand it, but he felt a heretofore unfamiliar, and yet compelling surge of need pulse through him, and before he could stop himself, he leaned forward to kiss those lips. The answering gasp, followed by more laughter that seemed to fill his own mouth and tickle against his palate, did not discourage him at all.

Efrosin's lips were soft and his tongue was slick and he didn't pull away from Dmitri's clumsy attempt, but rather deepened the kiss in a way that made Dmitri's toes curl and blood rush to his cock. For a confused moment he thought he was kissing an angel before he remembered that he was only kissing a prince. A free-floating, beautiful, powerful, laughing prince. Perhaps "only" was not quite the proper word.

"Lovely," Efrosin exclaimed, pulling away and licking his lips. "I hope you intend to ravish me, because I have always imagined it would be quite fun to be ravished. No one's ever tried it with me, alas." Efrosin frowned a little and licked his mouth. "You taste like dirt. It's delicious, though I've never enjoyed the taste of dirt before. How odd."

"You taste like clouds," Dmitri said, hoping it was a compliment.

"I ate quite a few during my journey to this tree," Efrosin said. "I…feel a bit strange. Quick. Kiss me again."

Dmitri, reminded of Efrosin's perilous flight, came to his senses, and while he was not willing to say that he would not kiss the prince again, he did think there were just a few things that should be accomplished first. "We must get you down."

Efrosin frowned, seeming much less intent on getting back to the earth now that he had company in the tree. "But you will kiss me again?"

"Once we're safe." Dmitri looked down to choose which limbs they should try, and immediately wished he hadn't. His head swirled with the distance between his body and the earth below. He'd never before climbed so high.

"Safe is such a thrilling state of being. I can't remember the last time I felt safe. Grip my hands," Efrosin said. "Don't let go."

Dmitri took Efrosin's smooth hands into

his own, and Efrosin began to shake with amusement again. "Your calluses tickle. Now hold tight. It will be fun."

"What will be?" Dmitri asked.

"Jump."

"What?"

"We are tied hand and foot, and you have hold of my hands. All will be well. Trust me."

It was surprisingly hard to trust laughing royalty. "We'll die. It's too far."

"Too far? What a silly notion."

DMITRI'S LAST THOUGHT when Efrosin kicked his feet out from under him with a strong swipe was, *At least I got to kiss him.* They tumbled into the air, crashing into branches below until Efrosin pushed off against the tree trunk, thrusting them both clear. It was only then Dmitri realized how slowly the ground rose up to meet them.

"Your weight to bring us down," Efrosin sang in his ear. "My levity to keep us from being quite smashed." There was more laughter, and then a curl of words in his ear, which, coupled with the rush of adrenaline coursing through his veins, made Dmitri's cock stiffen against the hard bone of Efrosin's hip. "And you will ravish me, won't you? Once we're on the ground. You promised. You're so handsome, and your hands are so big. I'm aquiver at the thought of you on me, in me, touching me—"

"Oh my God," Dmitri choked. "Do you speak to everyone who gets you down from trees this way?"

Efrosin's face twisted in horror. "Heavens no! Geoffry is nearly fifty years old. And the knights have never kissed me." The merriment was back, though, as Dmitri's feet alighted on the earth, and Efrosin's floated an inch above it. "But I would if the knights ever tried. Especially Sir Carlisle with that beard." Efrosin eyed him. "You are quite clean-shaven; have you ever thought of growing a beard?"

"I can't say I have."

"Beards are nice. Scratchy along the skin. I've noticed this quite often when Sir Carlisle has carried me, of course." Efrosin sighed dreamily, causing a strange, unpleasant feeling to twist in Dmitri's stomach.

So he kissed Efrosin again.

"Oh forget about beards," Efrosin breathed against Dmitri's lips. "The idiot never kissed me. Unlike very handsome, very," here Efrosin moved his hips against the length of Dmitri's cock, "hard you. This is rather lovely. Such a grand adventure. What a good birthday this is turning out to be."

Chapter Two

"YOU COULD ROPE me to that tree," Efrosin argued, bobbing along just above the woodland path beside the dark-haired, dark-eyed man. The man who had saved him from certain death and—better yet—had kissed him. "I wouldn't complain. It would be amusing, I'm sure, especially if you'll kiss me more and harder, and then do things to make the great pleasure descend."

The man gritted his teeth. "I said no." Still bound ankle to ankle, and wrist to wrist, so that Efrosin remained upright and floated along beside him not too far off the ground, the stranger pulled Efrosin with him down the path. Gnarled, ancient trees rose above them, twisted branches and thick leaves arching overhead and, in some places, blotting out the sky altogether.

"Whyever not?"

"I'm not about to tie you to a tree and pleasure you. We've known each other minutes. Is this how it's usually done in the royal court?"

"Perhaps? It seems quite likely."

"Well, don't you prefer it to be a little more…I don't know…romantic?"

Efrosin had never felt anything like this before. His body seemed to burn for the man's touch. Even his prick had woken from its slumber, and Efrosin chuckled over how odd it felt, heavy and aching in his trousers. What did his tutor tell him it was called? Ah yes. Lust. It was a rather divine and entertaining sensation, now that he knew it. He thought of how silly and desperate men behaved when consumed by it, and he hoped to be just as silly and desperate, indeed.

He licked his mouth to taste the man's spit still on his lips and stood up as straight as he could considering he was floating. "I am not a woman and nor are you. I do not need to be treated with kid gloves. Besides, what on earth could be more romantic than being taken in a hard and desperate manner by my rescuing prince?"

"I'm not a prince." His eyes were on Efrosin's mouth, and he stumbled a little over a tree root in his distraction. Efrosin licked his lips again with a slow swipe of his tongue. The man sighed. "Do stop that."

Efrosin knew that the man wanted to get back to the relative safety of his home, where there would be no risk of Efrosin floating into the sky. But Efrosin could tell that resolve was weakening. "You can have me in your house too," Efrosin said. "In fact, I insist upon it."

His rescuer appeared flustered. "Would you not like to get back to your castle?"

"But why? I'm having a great deal of fun

imagining what pleasures you're going to give me."

The man frowned, a wonderful little line forming between his eyes, and Efrosin marveled at his urge to lick it. He'd never understood the term "wanton" until now. This delirium was lovely.

"This is all very confusing. I left my house an hour ago to check my traps, and now I'm tied to a floating prince who is trying to get me to bugger him, and doesn't even know my name."

"Sir, must we exchange names? It seems too amusing to think that I might never know what you are called. Don't tell me."

"Dmitri," he said, frowning. "My name is Dmitri, and the idea of you not knowing does not amuse me at all."

Efrosin's mouth formed the name silently, and then he said it aloud. "Dmitri." The strangest thing happened—his toe dragged on the ground.

He tried it again. "Dmitri." And again

his toe brushed over roots and rocks as he was pulled along, tied as he was to Dmitri's wrist and ankle. He found he didn't want to laugh about it. That alone frightened him more than his brush with the earth. But then it passed, and he felt as free of weight as ever.

"Yes, that's my name. You say it like you've never heard it before. Is there no one else named Dmitri in all your kingdom?"

"Oh yes, quite a few. There's a stable hand, and a footman and a little snotty-nosed chimney sweep who coughs all the time. I rather dislike them all, actually. They always seem…wrong."

Dmitri listened to these revelations with a flat expression.

"Do you think it comes with the name?" Efrosin asked. "Are you a bit wrong?"

His lips curved into a small, rueful smile. "I should say so."

Efrosin said, "I don't know. You seem quite entirely right to me."

Dmitri ignored his appraisal. "Smoke

signals would be an option were the woods not so dangerously dry this spring. But a single spark could set the forest alight. No one comes by this way again until late summer. Even the river flows in the wrong direction, but perhaps we could send a note downstream anyway."

"Oh do end with all this worry. They will find me by and by. The wind could not have blown me too very far. What is the distance to Castle Goldenthal? Two leagues? Five?" How delightful the thought was of being such a long way from home.

"More like ten, sire, or so I hear. I'm afraid I don't know firsthand."

"Thrilling! My birthday party starts at seven. It seems that I will miss it, which is a shame. There were to be elephants and singers, and a brilliant cake made to look like a river. It was to be quite long and very blue."

Dmitri stared at him slack-jawed.

"But never mind. You can make it up to me with kisses." Efrosin leaned forward and took one. Dmitri's mouth was better than cake or elephants or singers. It was so good Efrosin didn't know how to categorize it or contain it. So, of course, he laughed, and Dmitri jerked away.

"But your people will be worried, surely. You wouldn't want them to think you're dead."

Efrosin waved his hand, dismissing that dull concern. "They are all quite funny when they're scared and cross, and they will search for me until they find me. Truly, there are likely knights looking for me even now. My dear Geoffry will probably be hanged if I am not found before nightfall, and judging by the sun, that is not so very long hence. Alas. He was a good servant. But let us think, ten leagues on horseback…they could be here any moment, could they not? You must hurry. If you're to ravish me, there is no time to lose."

Dmitri stared at him with an unfathomable emotion in his deep brown eyes, which were fringed with lashes so thick they would tickle wonderfully, Efrosin was quite sure, if applied to his neck, or wrist, or nether region.

"Geoffry—the man who pulls you from trees—shall be hanged?"

"Indeed he will, for the sin of losing me."

"And 'alas' is all you can say? You do not care for him at all?"

"Did I sound too blithe?" He concentrated on a somber expression. "It is a pity and if I could regret it, I most certainly would, but I can't. It's how I am." Efrosin tried hard not to sound so cheerful, but it was an impossible task. Perhaps he should apologize again? Sometimes that did the trick. "You have lovely eyes," he said instead. "And a beautiful mouth. Have you ever sucked a man's prick?"

Dmitri's sigh was unmistakably wistful before he seemed to remember himself. He cleared his throat. "No."

"Really? Am I the first to ask? In that

case, will you please be so kind as to suck mine?"

"Do you think of nothing else?" Dmitri asked, sounding frustrated, which was charming indeed.

"Oh quite. I truly never think of this at all. But you see, it is only now, with you, that I have ever felt quite exactly like this before. You are so very handsome."

"Am I?" He seemed surprised at this information, which made Efrosin's cock throb in delight.

"You are. Now, will you make good the promise of your lips on mine? That tree over there looks sturdy, and if you have more rope in your bag, then—"

"I have no more rope. Are all princes as brazen as you?"

"I haven't the faintest clue." Being jerked through the air was giving Efrosin rope burn, and if he was going to have rope burn, then he'd prefer it was from struggling to take Dmitri's dick whilst strapped to a tree, or perhaps a rock to hold him down. So he said as much.

"Listen, I am not going to screw your royal highness on the forest floor, nor bent over a boulder, nor tied to a tree. What you need is to get back to the castle."

Here in the mossy dim of the forest, with wood and moist earth filling his senses, Efrosin had never felt so far from home. But instead of fear, he felt a strange, warm comfort. "I think I'd quite like to stay here. For the time being, at least."

"Stay? Here?" Dmitri sputtered. "This is madness."

"It's my birthday after all. I've decided what I want. How much farther until we get to where you'll consent to kiss me again?"

Dmitri sighed as though he really wasn't eager to kiss him now, and that rather stung. "There. Just ahead."

Efrosin finally pulled his eyes from Dmitri's face and saw before them a tiny log cabin. It could not be more than one room.

Efrosin had never been inside a structure so small in his life. Just contemplating it set off peals of laughter.

Dmitri clenched his jaw. "Didn't your mother teach you manners?"

"I didn't have a mother."

Dmitri looked a bit shame-faced. "Of course. I'd forgotten the tales of your birth. I was…unkind. Forgive me."

Efrosin cast a glance from under his eyelashes. "Get me inside your hovel and do what you will with me, and I'll forgive you any unkindness."

Efrosin's dick had been hard since their first kiss, and as that was a sensation wholly unfamiliar to him—and thus utterly delightful—he was eager for his life-long chastity to come to an end. He summoned his straightest face, though he could feel it was softened with mirth, and said, "As your prince, I command you, take me into your home and defile me."

Despite his laughter, he thought it must

have done the trick, because Dmitri grabbed hold of his waist and quickly led him to the cabin.

AS DMITRI THRUST open the door to his home, he wondered again if this was some bizarre dream he'd fallen into. The lurid turn it had taken was not unusual, for he was but twenty and quite lonely. He often dreamed of beautiful men coming to his cabin for the sole purpose of bending over for him.

There had even been a very queer dream similar in its lack of believability wherein a young, beautiful woman had arrived at his door with an apple in her outstretched hand. When he took it from her, to his great astonishment, she hitched her skirts up, and he'd spied a long, hard, curved cock instead of the fuzzy mound he'd been expecting. He'd clutched that velvet prick in his hand

and tossed the witch's skirts up to her shoulders, rubbing his own hardness all along her strong, flat stomach, until he'd woken up gasping and sticky.

Perhaps if he did as Prince Efrosin asked, the dream would end and he'd wake the same way he always did—physically sated but utterly alone. He wavered between pinching himself awake, and tossing Efrosin on the bed to fuck him silly the way he'd been begging for the whole walk home.

Did Dmitri really want to risk that he might never dream this particular dream again? Efrosin was beautiful, and pulling at him impatiently where they were attached ankle-to-ankle and wrist-to-wrist. The prince wanted it—wanted him. Dmitri's cock throbbed in answer. But if it wasn't a dream, what of the king's search party? How would it look to be found buggering the prince? Would they execute him on the spot for such an offense?

Efrosin clapped his hands, his eyes glowing with amusement. "This is smaller than my old dollhouse."

Dmitri shut the door behind them and took in the room with its wood stove and the square table his father had built to the right. A rocking chair sat next to the only window on the left. In the middle, a trap door led down to the root cellar where he stored his cured meats and vegetables. With a critical eye, he gazed at the far wall and the shelf full of his most treasured items—books—and the rather threadbare mattress atop the wooden bed with tall, smooth, sanded posts, in which his mother had conceived Dmitri.

Was it truly so small? To Dmitri it was the world. Who could have need for more? "Well, it's only me."

"You're alone here?" Efrosin seemed enlivened by such a concept. "How incredibly novel."

"Rather old hat, actually."

Dmitri started every day alone, went to bed every night alone, and spent all but fourteen or fifteen hours a year completely on his own. To say that he was lonely did not fully capture the immensity of his situation. It suddenly hit him that if this was not a dream—and he was rather convinced that it was not—then he only had a few hours of Efrosin's company. Who knew when someone might visit again? Much less someone like Efrosin. He should make the most of it.

"I'm generally not allowed to be alone," Efrosin said, tugging at the links between them, urging Dmitri deeper into the room.

"Why?"

"I might float away, of course. All it takes is someone leaving a window open, and an inopportune waft of air from, say, a lady passing by the door waving a fan, and *voila*, I'm off on an adventure that could end in death."

Dmitri believed that Efrosin sounded much too cheerful about that, but then he sounded cheerful about everything.

"Have you ever imagined what it might be like to see the stars in their own dark habitat?" Efrosin said. "I suspect it is my destiny to do so. For I could float that high, I'm quite sure. The problem is suffocating before I get there. The air gets so very thin." Efrosin looked around again, his babbling ceasing for a moment. "The bed will do, I suppose. Do be romantic: tie me to the posts and cut off my clothes."

Dmitri was sorely tempted as he imagined what the prince's naked body might look like. "Won't you need them for the trip home?"

"They can wrap me in blankets until they reach the river, at which point I'll happily swim the rest of the way."

"Ten leagues is much too far to swim."

"Says who? Go on now, tie me up and cut my clothes off. I feel as though I'll burst if I'm forced to wait a moment longer."

Frowning, Dmitri reached for the knife he had tucked in his boot and quickly cut the rope that had lashed them ankle-to-ankle. He watched in awe as Efrosin giggled and floated feet-first toward the low ceiling, still attached at Dmitri's wrist.

Dmitri didn't know if he should try to pull him back down again or not, but Efrosin jerked on their attached arms and said, "Cut that one too then. Or the blood will all go to my head, and that gives me such a terribly funny headache."

Dmitri cut him free and stared as Efrosin spun round, twirling until his feet touched the ceiling, and then pushed off again, sliding through the air like an eel in water. He reached out with his hands to run his fingers over the walls and the shelf of books before rising back to the ceiling again, where he repeated the push-off and continued his exploration.

Efrosin gripped the edge of the book shelf to read the titles. "Science, science, history, farming, history. Yawn, yawn, yawn, each yawnier than the last. Where are the novels? Where are the torrid stories of illicit coupling? Your mind must be sorely lacking in key areas. No wonder you didn't understand the romance of our situation in the woods." Efrosin's laughter took the sting from his words, and he pushed off the shelf with enough force to catapult through the air until he grabbed the post at the foot of the bed. He held on with one hand, and with the other began to remove his clothes. "Such a silly Dmitri."

Efrosin's body sank about a foot suddenly, and his brow furrowed, but then he was back to floating near the ceiling as his hand gripped the post. He kicked off again, and he hooked a leg around the post, so that it appeared as though he was standing upright in mid-air on one pointed toe.

"Shall we then?" he asked.

Chapter Three

DMITRI'S MOUTH WENT dry as he watched Efrosin's long, lovely fingers open the buttons of his shirt, revealing creamy skin and small, budded nipples. Dmitri could not tear his eyes away from the light golden hair on Efrosin's chest that was followed by a thicker patch leading from his navel down to where his hand was now working to open the drawstring of his white and silver-edged pants.

Dmitri licked his lips at the sight of the wet spot staining the silk. *Are you really going to bugger him?* Incredulity and common sense threatened to overpower his lust. *It's a dream.*

A strange but powerful dream. Whyever not? When you wake, you'll be quite sorry if you don't.

But he was not convinced. There was nothing aside from the unlikeliness of it all that spoke to it being a dream.

"Dmitri," Efrosin said, and he sank down the bed post a bit. "I order you under penalty of death to rid me of my cursed virginity." His laughter and inability to say it with a straight face didn't impress anything upon Dmitri other than Prince Efrosin was not afraid to be debauched.

It's what he wants. And you're his subject—of course you'll obey.

But being Efrosin's subject was less of a consideration to Dmitri than the knowledge that he might never get a chance to screw someone again, much less someone as beautiful as Efrosin. And for some unknown reason, Efrosin seemed to feel the same way, given how desperate he was to be plowed immediately and in any way possible, and that need pulled at Dmitri, winding through him like siren song, impossible to ignore.

Dumbstruck, Dmitri watched as Efrosin kicked his pants free, and his body—too masculine to be called delicate, but still supple and slender—was exposed in its considerable beauty. Dmitri's blood thundered at the vision of Efrosin's cock, gorgeous and nothing like Dmitri's own. It was flushed and long, with a rosy, thick head and a slimmer girth. His thighs were sprinkled with that same golden hair from his chest, and his arms and legs were muscular but lean.

"Don't you—do you not think we should—" Dmitri didn't get any more words out, his cock aching and pushing against his breeches painfully. "Oh God forgive me," he muttered, tearing his shirt over his head and casting it aside, his eyes greedily raking over Efrosin's form, taking in every inch of him that was on offer. He ripped open his pants, kicked them off and lunged at Efrosin.

"Forget God," Efrosin said, eyes alight with excitement, and deep laughter rumbling up from his chest. "What has He got to do with anything?"

Dmitri had no thought left in his mind to be appalled at the blasphemy as he grabbed hold of Efrosin's floating ankle and jerked him effortlessly down. He gasped, finding Efrosin quite firm and solid in his arms. His skin was softer than he'd thought possible, but his muscles and bones stronger than expected. Efrosin's laughter was intoxicating against Dmitri's mouth, bubbling into his throat and filling him with a giddy need that felt too good to bear.

"Brilliant," Efrosin cried, as Dmitri threw Efrosin to the bed and captured him there beneath his own body.

Bloody brilliant indeed. He attached his mouth to Efrosin's neck, biting gently, and smoothed his palms over every bit of skin he could. Now, if only he wouldn't lose his mind and shoot his seed too soon. His skin tingled and his prick throbbed with his heartbeat as desperation drove him onward, overcome with a need to fulfill Efrosin's urgent lust, dimly aware beneath his own screaming desire that he would only be truly content again upon Efrosin's satisfaction.

EFROSIN HAD NEVER felt such a delicious sense of weight. Even when he'd been held down forcibly in the past, it had not been like this. Of course it hadn't. He'd never been naked, hard and rutting together with another man in desperate, grasping need. Dmitri was bigger than he was. Taller, and could cover him with his entire body, which made Efrosin feel that most delightful thing of all—safe.

As lust-soaked moans filled the tiny room, Dmitri pinned him, their arms and legs tangled, mouths open and tasting everything in reach. Efrosin quickly lost track of whether his mouth was on Dmitri's arm, neck, cheek, ear or chest, only knowing that Dmitri tasted of earth and skin. It was good—so very good—that Efrosin wasn't even laughing. But before he could fully realize that oddity, he was again enraptured by the intense sensation of flesh sliding on flesh, cock against cock.

Efrosin had never had a moment of modesty in his life, but rocking beneath Dmitri, he suddenly felt shy and hid his face in the crook of Dmitri's neck. He tingled, aware of where his body rubbed against Dmitri's, and he swallowed against the strange thickness in his throat that felt like trapped laughter. Why did it not come out? Usually, no sooner did it bubble up in him than it spilled free.

Dmitri was also clearly overwhelmed, moaning most delightfully as his hands ran everywhere over Efrosin's body, his mouth following, wet and hot, kissing Efrosin's neck and sucking his collar bone before biting down against Efrosin's pink, tight nipple. Dmitri's mouth came back to fit against Efrosin's own, his tongue licking lightly at his lips, until Efrosin grabbed him by the nape of his neck, and forced him into a harder, deeper kiss.

Dmitri groaned and gasped, clasping Efrosin tighter, his fingers digging into Efrosin's buttocks, pulling their hips flush. Efrosin threw his legs around Dmitri's heaving back, hooking his ankles and holding on as best he could as they writhed together.

His tutor had educated him on the theory, but the reality was beyond Efrosin's imagining. There was no space between them at all, and Efrosin's world narrowed down to their desperate grappling, the scent of their lust permeating the air between them as they grunted and whimpered. Efrosin's pulse beat in his ears, and he quivered as he felt their cocks throb against each other, foreshadowing oncoming climaxes that promised to be so much that Efrosin quaked in fear and longing for it.

His balls drew up with a shocking wrench in his gut, and he held on tight, tangling his fingers into Dmitri's dark hair, kissing him again, running the tip of his tongue along the roof of Dmitri's mouth. And then, faster than he wanted, it was over.

Efrosin arched, his toes flexed, and as his cock rubbed alongside Dmitri's, slick with their sweat and over-eager seed, he felt something hard and heavy drag up through him, as if from an internal depth he never knew existed. It settled in his gut, burning and weighing there, before he screamed.

Afraid and ecstatic, he clawed at Dmitri's back and shoulders as he pulsed, his cock spurting and his eyes locked in shock on Dmitri's own. It was like nothing he'd ever felt before, and he shook, wondering if his heart would stop from immense wonder.

Dmitri kissed him again, a sharp moan in his throat, more like a desperate plea, before thrusting his prick against Efrosin's stomach, now sloppy with Efrosin's spendings. He jerked, shaking on top of Efrosin as bursts of wet heat shot over Efrosin's stomach and chest.

"Oh," Efrosin cried, still shivering and watching in delight as Dmitri's face contorted in pleasure. "Was that…is that…?" Efrosin was breathless. He felt addled, confused and utterly deconstructed.

Dmitri pulled back to look at the mess between their bodies and, with a groan, unloaded a last, surprising shot of seed onto Efrosin's stomach. Dmitri's pupils were blown wide and he stared open-mouthed and panting at Efrosin.

"That was ravishing then? No wonder it is so highly recommended by romance novels and plays."

Dmitri nodded, wordless and still shuddering.

Efrosin's mouth seemed to have found words, even if his mind was yet lost in orbit.

He shifted beneath Dmitri, a subtle shivery tingle filling him up again like a tide or eddy, and then pulling away, leaving him breathless and limp. "It was frightening, but really quite wonderful. Is the end always like that? I was afraid I'd come apart. I almost could not bear it."

Dmitri's mouth twisted into a smile, and he laughed softly, ducking his head to lick and kiss at Efrosin's sweaty neck. He pushed Efrosin's hands, which floated in the air beside them, down to the mattress. "Did you not know?" he asked, clearly amused, his dark eyes sparkling.

"I...no. I've seen it before and watched other men crumble and cry out under its power, but..." Efrosin trailed off, blood rushing down to his still-sensitive prick, stiffening it again, at the memory of what he'd just felt, what they'd done.

"Watched?" Dmitri asked. "Is it not a private thing elsewhere in the kingdom? My parents gave the idea that taking one's pleasure in another's body, or even one's own, wasn't something done in front of spectators."

Efrosin pulled one hand free of Dmitri's restraining grasp and flapped it in the air, waving the words away. "No, it's private. Though I have heard rumors of brothels where…but no, it is private." Here Efrosin felt a shocking thing—heat that rose over his chest, up into his cheeks, and burned his ears. Was this shame? He'd never felt anything quite like it before. "However, men and women do not often check their rafters whilst seeking release."

Dmitri's brows lowered and he shifted his body, the sticky mess between them smearing. "Do you not know that's wrong?" His voice seemed to hold no censure, however.

"I was curious. But my prick never did those things." Efrosin remembered how funny it had seemed, the urgent rutting, the cries and wails, the silly faces as the end drew near, and the mess. He'd been unable to refrain from busting out in chortles on more than one occasion and he'd had to dodge flying slippers and boots as he bobbed down the hallways of the castle, ringing with laughter at what he'd seen.

Now, feeling Dmitri's weight holding him down, and still vibrating with the resounding pleasure they'd taken together, it did not seem so funny. Efrosin did not know what to make of that. He felt almost afraid, but when he looked up into Dmitri's face, seeing no anger or malice there, and felt Dmitri's cock lengthening between their bodies again, he felt in his bones that he was safe.

"You've never…?" Here Dmitri flung his fist back and forth in a crude gesture to illustrate self-pleasure.

Efrosin shook his head. He'd always been vaguely curious as to why his cock didn't seem to function as others' did, and so Efrosin had asked Geoffry about it once. The old dear, sputtering and looking red in the face, had answered, "It's a rather grave undertaking at heart, sire. A primal urge. Quite deep. Perhaps your affliction doesn't allow you to reach down to such base impulses."

All it had taken was one kiss from Dmitri, Efrosin realized, and his dormant, earthly desires had risen in him fast and ruthlessly hard. He'd been quite…what was the word he'd heard the knights use? He'd been quite the trollop.

Dmitri stroked a finger over Efrosin's lips. "That was the first time you've ever spent?"

"It was."

"You looked so beautiful."

"As did you. Have you felt it before?"

Dmitri laughed, a warm chuckle that spread through Efrosin until he was laughing, too. "More times than I could count. But never with another. It's different with you."

Efrosin laughed harder, as if the chuckle

he'd caught from Dmitri had reminded him of his nature. His body started to rise, his feet and head and hands floating up where Dmitri did not hold them down. Dmitri's hand slid between them and grasped their cocks together, squeezing. Efrosin gurgled in a combination of renewed lust and amusement.

"You begged me to bugger you," Dmitri said, his voice thick with want again.

"Oh please do. The knights who take each other that way cry out so loudly. Given how often they do it, and how they squirm and beg for more, it must be ever so wonderful. Do you think I will squirm? Shall I beg?"

Dmitri bit his lip, his eyes going even darker with lust, and then he shifted off Efrosin to lean over the side of the bed, rummaging for something under it. As he did, Efrosin rose up with a stomach-lurching swiftness, but Dmitri grabbed him by the ankle and pulled him back to the bed, holding a jar in his other hand.

"Of course, I should warn you," Dmitri said, as he reached for edge of the blanket their rutting had wadded up against the side of the bed. "I've never buggered anyone before."

He held Efrosin down with one palm flat on Efrosin's chest as he used the other hand to shove one end of the blanket between the mattress and the wall, and then, moving away, he pulled the blanket taut over Efrosin's upper body to hold him in place. He tucked the other side under the mattress, and then leaned back, double-checking his handiwork.

Efrosin's arms and legs floated up, but his body was trapped against the soft, worn mattress. The blanket was not of a fine material, and it rubbed Efrosin's hard nipples roughly, making him want to rub against it and simultaneously move away. He squirmed to test its limits, surprised when the binding held.

He felt contained and vulnerable, with his hard cock and twitching balls bare below the blanket. Dmitri's eyes were fixed there, his tongue running over his lips as he knelt between Efrosin's floating legs and seemed to study Efrosin's prick and exposed anus.

"Have you never put your fingers there?" Dmitri asked, and Efrosin shuddered at the thick, muddy sound in his voice.

"Yes," Efrosin said. "It hurt. And I couldn't stop laughing. It was too funny. I stopped at two."

"You know enough from watching, I assume, to understand what I must do?"

Efrosin nodded, though at the moment his mind was blank, and he could recall nothing other than the fact that he was bound naked to a bed, cock and balls alive in a way he'd never known, and his asshole flexing in a distracting, tingling way under Dmitri's gaze.

Dmitri opened the bottle and spread the slick contents over the fingers of his right hand, and then over his cock, before pouring some into his palm. Efrosin bucked, his heart thudding, his legs quivering in the air next to Dmitri's shoulders, and then Dmitri leaned forward, two fingers pushing tentatively at Efrosin's asshole. He rubbed and pushed until Efrosin felt his pucker give way and take one finger in.

It was a sharp sensation, a burning stretch, and then Efrosin felt his body adjust, a softening and welcoming that took place deep within Efrosin's soul, and he moaned. Dmitri's second finger worked in, and Efrosin reached out with his hands, fingers wriggling in the air, as he rotated his hips and pushed down, forcing Dmitri's fingers farther inside.

Efrosin bit his lip, and Dmitri's mouth parted, his eyes wide and hot, his firm chest heaving with lust. "Is this all right?" Dmitri asked.

A lust for more welled within Efrosin, and he whimpered and begged with his body.

He squirmed down on Dmitri's twisting fingers, heart pounding, his cock rigid with urgency. Dmitri's eyes sparkled. "I know what you need," he whispered, and Efrosin felt flooded with relief when Dmitri edged a third finger into him, drawing his asshole breathtakingly tight.

"Dmitri," he whimpered.

As Dmitri fucked him with his fingers, Efrosin rolled his head back and forth, surprised by the sudden weight of it against the soft pillow, but then the thought was gone. He cried out and kicked his feet in the air, overcome by a sensation he'd not known to expect. Then it came again. Efrosin gasped, his sight blurred, and sweat broke out over his skin as he writhed in the throes of ecstasy.

Dmitri had hooked his fingers and touched something, something that was the very meaning of deep, the very opposite of airy, and Efrosin rode Dmitri's fingers wantonly, pushing his ass at him, begging to feel it once more. He kicked at the air, his body tensing and clenching around Dmitri's solid, working fingers as the fantastic feeling exploded through him, shocking him with depths of pleasure.

With a groan, Dmitri muttered, "Can't wait. You need it. You need it so much."

Efrosin's eyes squeezed shut. His heart pounded, his legs floated and shook, and he tangled his hands into his own hair, tugging hard to keep from falling so heavily into sensation and lust that he'd never crawl out. Then he felt the horrible sensation of Dmitri's fingers pulling free, and just as he cried out, bereft, there came a pressure and stretch—so thick, so big—that nearly blew off the top of his head.

He pushed down to accept Dmitri's prick, arching his neck as he cried out. He felt the burn and stretch at his asshole, and then the pain seemed to drill into him, touching him somewhere inexplicably deep, like an undiscovered mine inside him was bleeding jewels.

Efrosin threw his legs around Dmitri's back, jerking and crying out as the thick head of Dmitri's cock pushed past his ring of muscle with a pop that jolted him to the core. Then there was a thick, slow, deep slide in, and Efrosin pounded Dmitri's back with his heels and squirmed, his body spasming and releasing as he took Dmitri's length.

Efrosin had never felt so unfathomable, and yet when he opened his eyes, his breath caught on a whimper. Dmitri was there, his cheeks flushed, and tender understanding on his face.

"There, there," Dmitri whispered, bent over, holding Efrosin's arms down. "It's almost in. Bear down, my Efrosin. Take me."

Efrosin felt a hot prickle at the back of his neck, and then a sweeping, consuming, burning chill that made him quake all over with mad, mad lust. He threw his hips up to meet Dmitri, slamming Dmitri's cock in to the root, clawing at Dmitri's back to better grasp his solidity.

"Oh God," Dmitri groaned, his eyes screwed tight as he lunged forward, hands gripping the pillow underneath Efrosin's head. He muttered, "I've never…" And he froze, his face flushed with effort, flexed into Efrosin's body, stretching him open.

Efrosin squeezed his ass around Dmitri and he bit his own lip, digging his heels into Dmitri's back. Dmitri's cock felt heavy, a thick weight where it stretched Efrosin's inner walls and brushed against him deep inside where he had never been touched before. The thought alone made him whimper again. He shifted beneath Dmitri's weight, digging his prick into the scratchy trail of dark hair beneath Dmitri's navel.

"Good God," Dmitri cried, his body straining over Efrosin, holding so perfectly still.

When Efrosin brought his arms around Dmitri's neck, they stared into each other's eyes. Their breath mingled as their bodies pulsed and ached where they joined, and Efrosin didn't feel like laughing. Not even a little bit.

DMITRI KNEW IF he moved he'd spurt his seed. He'd never been inside another man before. Never known the sweet, delicious tightness and heat. Never felt the fast thud of another's pulse around his cock, nor watched another's eyes open wide with feverish need as he pushed into their ass and held there, trembling.

It was that need most of all that had him hanging on the edge. His very bones seemed compelled to answer its call, and yet to move would surely make him spend. It was a desperate paradox that left him sweating and moaning.

That it was Efrosin—a man more beautiful than any Dmitri had ever seen, a prince troubled with an astounding lightness of body that made Dmitri feel as though his cock was thrust into a surprisingly solid ghost—only served to drive him closer to the edge. Somehow, despite the heavy scent of their previous coupling, Dmitri thought he could still smell the sharp odor of clouds in Efrosin's hair and taste it on his skin.

He leaned forward, sucking on Efrosin's earlobe, groaning as Efrosin squirmed under him, eyes rolled back in his head, pulling against Dmitri with his hands, urging him on with his body. As moments passed and Efrosin's body screamed for more, Dmitri felt himself slip until he was clinging to the edge.

Efrosin moaned low in his throat and met Dmitri's eyes, begging, "Please! More!"

Unable to deny such outright need from Efrosin, Dmitri rolled his hips, fucking deeply with a powerful thrust. Grimacing, he plummeted over into ecstasy. He twisted in Efrosin's embrace as he yelled and shook, shooting his seed deep into Efrosin's body.

Efrosin jerked. "Oh my God! Oh it is so much!" His voice was laced with confusion and want.

Dmitri didn't pull out, driven by his need to see Efrosin through to the end. Everything about Efrosin's wide eyes and open, red mouth told Dmitri that their coupling must go on, and his own desire rose again to meet that requirement. Dmitri had been so alone, and now he was tangled with another, moving as one, commingled fluids and breath making him quiver. He wasn't ready for it to be over either. He hunched and thrust, driving his too-sensitive and still-hard cock into Efrosin's tight, hot, slick hole, now made sloppy by Dmitri's seed. Both of them crowed and clawed, hunger once again consuming them.

Efrosin felt heavier in Dmitri's arms, and Dmitri leaned forward to kiss his crooning mouth, shocked to see a depth in Efrosin's eyes that hadn't been there before. As he plunged into Efrosin's body, swiveling his hips, hitting every angle, he knew that he'd rubbed the sweet spot inside when Efrosin's legs kicked out on reflex, and his fingers clenched on Dmitri's shoulders, nails digging in.

Then there was the sound—the noise of sheer wonder and terror combined—that tore out of Efrosin at those times, and Dmitri almost slowed his rapid assault on Efrosin's hole, thinking that it must be rather scary for him to feel these things when he'd never even known the pleasure of his own hand.

But he did not. He couldn't. His hips did not slow, his pounding did not ease, and Efrosin's screams of, "Yes! Yes! Please!" overrode the trepidation that Dmitri saw in his eyes. Understanding Efrosin's need for more was greater than any need for comfort. Consumed, he slammed into Efrosin, seeking their climax.

Efrosin didn't last long, not once Dmitri found the right angle, and he rammed the thick head of his cock over the place within again and again until Efrosin struggled in his arms, desperately trying to get his hand between their bodies. Before he could, Efrosin stiffened, crowed with a startled bliss, and his ass spasmed and clenched around Dmitri.

Efrosin's seed splashed against Dmitri's stomach and, looking between them, Dmitri saw another great glob of it land across the top of the blanket that was still anchoring Efrosin down. Dmitri kissed Efrosin's mouth, swallowing the sound of his cries, and pulled back to gaze into his blue, surprised eyes, crinkled at the edges with such ready joy. Dmitri gave up to that sweetness, cocking his hips and thrusting hard. He yelled in delight as his cock convulsed inside Efrosin, filling his hole with seed again, and he shook all over as the ecstasy raked over him, leaving him feeling exposed, like earth freshly tilled.

Dmitri tore the blanket away before collapsing on top of Efrosin, who reached up with one shaking hand to stroke Dmitri's hair as they rested, skin to skin, trembling, and still joined below.

Dmitri knew that what he felt was impossible, but having been alone for so long, he found he couldn't help himself. In his heart, where it had no business and did not belong, Efrosin had planted a seed as surely as Dmitri had loaded Efrosin with his own. It was a seed of friendship, affection and—worst of all—love. Dmitri knew then, kissing Efrosin's red, bitten lips, and feeling his body clench and tremble around him, that this seed would be his undoing.

After Dmitri wiped their spendings from Efrosin's stomach and between his legs, he realized Efrosin began to rise up again, a steady increase in his flotation until he was difficult for Dmitri to hold down. It was as if Efrosin's body longed for the sky.

"That was so beautiful," Efrosin said, eyes shining and his lips ruby red from their kisses. There were stains on his neck and jaw too, from where Dmitri had bitten and sucked, and he looked like a debauched angel, especially with his arms and legs levitating effortlessly. The only thing holding him against the bed now was Dmitri's strong arms around his waist.

"When they find me, you must come home with me," Efrosin said. "You could be my consort, my lover, my pretty peacock of perpetual penile pleasure." And he laughed, a tinkling sound more like what Dmitri had heard from up in the tree, and not the deep rumbling one that had filled them both when Dmitri had been buried deep inside him. "You must come. I don't think I can live without you."

Dmitri thought he sounded anything but sincere, but understood Efrosin probably couldn't sound sincere about something as serious as death if he tried. "I can't."

"Of course you can. You have nothing but a hovel here. I can give you a castle, and servants, and anything your heart desires.

You'll come stay with me, sleep in my bed, drag me down from the ceiling to have your wicked way with me, make me heavy with your seed and then drop off to a snoring sleep as I watch you from above like a guardian angel. No one would ever dare bother you. You'd have a place by my side and my father would have to accept you. Wouldn't that be lovely? How can you say no?"

"Because I can't. I can't leave my land— my father's land."

"For heaven's sake, whyever not?"

Dmitri touched Efrosin's handsome face, his thumb tracing the light line of his golden stubble, and told his story.

Chapter Four

ONCE UPON A time, there was an old woodcutter who took a pretty, young wife to live with him deep in the forest. Always eager to fulfill the needs of good-hearted people, the earth fairies saw to it that the woodcutter and his wife had all that they could ever want with their small but fruitful garden, a lake for fishing and woods for trapping game.

In the midst of so much plenty, the differences between them, given his old age and her youthful bloom, seemed unimportant, and they were quite happy there, alone amid the trees on their several acres of land.

Eventually, the young wife let the old woodcutter know that she was with child. Both of them were quite filled to the brim with joy. The earth fairies seemed to share their happiness, for the garden was never so prolific as it was that summer. As autumn approached, the wife's belly swelled with the melons from the furrows, and not wanting any time apart from his lovely bride, the woodcutter gave up his trade, happily settling into domestic bliss in the last years of his life.

But the birth did not go well.

The child was too well rooted in the mother, and when his head finally came forth, he could only be persuaded from her body with a giant tug from the woodcutter. The wife screamed, and the babe came free of her like a plant ripped from the earth. But then the blood began, and the fever, and the woodcutter despaired.

To his great astonishment, five fairies, all

grown as tall as men, with skin the color of sun-baked mud and eyes dark as dirt, filed into the cabin to tend to his wife. The woodcutter was not sure if they were male or female, or perhaps a bit of both. He watched the fairies argue amongst themselves in a language he didn't know, fear keeping his tongue silent. No magic, nor medicine, nor herb given seemed to help his wife.

Then, in words he could understand, the fairies told the woodcutter what he must do next. Reluctant, but desperate to save his wife, he saddled his old horse and left her and the infant in the care of the fae, going, as the fairies had insisted, in search of a very old midwife.

"She lives on the boundary between the known world and the mountains," one fairy had said. "Tell her we send for her. Bound as we are to our land, we cannot leave. Call her Mother. Be polite and plead with her. Do whatever you must. Ignore her cruelty. If you love your wife, do as we say."

Not even half a day into his journey, the woodcutter rounded a bend and found an old, bent woman waiting in the middle of the road. She leaned on a staff and a blackbird perched on her shoulder. The woodcutter eagerly approached. "Perhaps you can help me, good lady. I desperately seek a woman who lives at the end of the world. Might you know of her?"

The old woman's eyes glinted, and the bird on her shoulder let out a loud caw. "A midwife, perhaps? For a wife sick with childbed fever?"

The woodcutter couldn't believe his ears. "Yes. The fae of the earth have sent me to find one called Mother."

The woman licked her dirty lips. "I am the Mother you seek. But this child should not live."

"He is but a babe, my only son. Please, you must help my Dmitri and my wife."

The old woman smiled, revealing teeth as black as coal. "Dmitri, you say? Lover of the earth. 'Tis a lucky name, and I'm feeling merciful. I will only punish those at fault on this day. Lead the way, fool."

Upon returning to the cabin, the midwife took in the squalling child held against his mother's fevered tit. The five fae fell to their knees before her, beseeching. She tsked sharply, and they cowered. Then the old woman uttered something that made the fae blanch in terror, crying out as one before bursting into flame.

The woodcutter ran for a bucket of water, but the fire burned itself out with a whoosh, leaving only traces of fine ash where the fairies had been. He stood before his wife and child, arms outstretched to shield them from the woman. "I beg you, do not harm them."

The crone cackled. "Do not fret. I will cure her. But first give me the child. No harm will come to him," the witch said. For yes, she was a witch, of course she was.

Terrified, the woodcutter passed his

small son into the witch's dirty hands. She whispered in his ear and cackled to herself before turning to the man. "This one will be bound to the land. Never will he leave until death claims him."

The woodcutter wordlessly accepted the price, clutching his wife's hot fingers. They had all that they wanted, and so long as his wife and the babe lived, they had no need for more.

The witch kissed the boy's head before putting him back to his mother's breast. She touched the woodcutter's wife upon each eyelid and spoke in unintelligible words. Then she turned her back and walked from the house, never to be seen or heard from again.

From that time forward, the woodcutter's child was bound by his father's bargain. The father and mother saw it as a price well worth paying, but the son saw it as a curse, and resented it every day of his life.

EFROSIN'S EYES SHONE and he clapped at the telling. Despite that it was his own tale of woe, Dmitri wondered at the sense of accomplishment it gave him to receive an ovation from a prince. Surely Efrosin had heard better stories than his during the parties hosted by the king at the castle, and yet Efrosin's enthusiasm was undampened by any snobbery.

Efrosin said breathlessly, "What a wonderful story. Where are your parents now?" He snuggled into Dmitri's arms, Dmitri's weight keeping him safe from floating.

"They died five years ago. A traveling salesman brought the pox." It was strange to speak of it, being so alone as he was through the years. The grief flared hollowly in his chest.

"Oh how exciting! And what did you do

with their bodies?"

Dmitri frowned. "I buried them."

Efrosin's lips twitched. "Grave digging. That sounds quite—oh wait a moment. I am sure Geoffry covered this in his teachings. Laughing about death offends people, you see…so, let me think. Oh yes, I am to look sad—" Here Efrosin's face contorted in a terrible attempt at misery. "And I am to say, 'My greatest sympathy for your loss, dear citizen'." Efrosin grinned. "There. Do you feel much better now?"

Dmitri narrowed his eyes and said, "No. I shall never feel 'much better' about digging a grave for my parents' bodies."

Efrosin seemed to ponder this. "I suppose not. Tell me, have you ever tried to leave your land?"

"Not until my parents died. While they were alive, they needed me here. But once they were naught but a memory, I resolved to leave this place and journey to the worlds I've only read about in my books. Yet I could not due to my father's promise. I am truly bound." The heaviness in his chest made it difficult to draw breath.

For a moment, Efrosin appeared genuinely troubled, but the graveness of his expression soon flickered into a smile. "Then let's talk about something else. What of the lake near your cabin, and the river that feeds it? Does it flow from the castle? If so, should no one come for me, when I wish to take my leave I could happily swim home. I quite like to swim. In fact, it is fair to say that I love swimming more than life."

"Of course you'll want to be going." Dmitri sighed. He touched Efrosin's neck, feeling Efrosin's pulse against his fingertips. He hated that this would be the end of it, though of course it must be.

Efrosin peered at him curiously and asked with a tone of pure wonder, as though the idea of what he was asking was somehow thrilling, "Do you get awfully lonely then?"

"Lonely? When I'm alone, confined here

to this parcel of land, for all of my days? Whyever would I be lonely?" Dmitri could not keep the bitterness from his tongue. He was tempted to bend down and kiss Efrosin's mouth to replace it with the taste of clouds again.

"And no servants at all? However do you eat?"

"I hunt and fish, and grow a bit of food. Sometimes, if I'm lucky, someone will happen by and trade for some seeds or fresh fruit."

"Ah, I see. Well," Efrosin, said airily, and looking as though it was a contest and he intended to win. "I grow lonely too."

"You? A prince at a castle bustling with servants, knights and diplomats? You've already said that you are always surrounded by people."

"True. I am. But none of them like me. I don't have any friends," he said gaily. "Who wants to play with a child who floats away? The boys could not play ball with me, or go riding or hunting. They tried to strap me to a horse once, but it was for naught. He couldn't feel my weight on his back and ran wild. Oh what a terrifying thrill that was. I laughed so hard I threw up."

Dmitri had to stifle a chortle at the picture that brought to mind even as he felt an answering pang at Efrosin's lack of friendship. He would be the finest friend Efrosin ever had if only given the chance.

"Do you ride?" Efrosin asked.

"I had a horse…but she died a few years before my father passed away. We never had need of another." Before Efrosin could ask what had come of the old horse's body, Dmitri continued on, "But we were speaking of you, not me. Surely there were girls at least?"

"Girls? Oh certainly, but who wants to braid my hair and put in ribbons when I float to the ceiling half the time? And they hated that I was prettier than they."

Given that Dmitri had at first believed

Efrosin to be an entangled angel, there was no room for bringing Efrosin's ego down a peg. He truly did possess an otherworldly beauty. "Well, you certainly don't seem sad about it."

"That's the curse, you see. I couldn't feel sad if I tried. It's quite…well, sad really."

"I actually meant maidens and courtesans to please you."

"Oh, pleasing me. I've told you, until you kissed me, I could not be pleased. And even if they tried, they weigh so little it would require that they tie me down, and it grows so tiresome being tied down. Unable to move or go wherever you wish. The constant rope burn. Can you even imagine?"

"Yes, my prince. I understand not being able to go wherever you wish," Dmitri said, smiling at the bright outrage that glowed alongside an odd glee in Efrosin's expression. "Though, I admit, you have me beaten with the rope burn. I do not have that particular trouble. I suppose I should be grateful for small mercies."

Despite it all, Efrosin's eyes sparkled with joy, and he wriggled beneath Dmitri. "Oh I won! I truly won. I am sadder than you!"

Dmitri didn't have the heart to tell him that he hadn't actually won, and that Dmitri was quite sure burying his parents in a plot by the house—digging the graves with his own two hands before returning his parents to their beloved land—surely trumped some rope burn, and not having friends to play with, or girls to braid his hair. Yet he found himself absently rubbing Efrosin's wrist where the rope had chafed the soft skin.

"Dmitri," Efrosin said, and then sucked in a breath as his floating hands dropped down to the mattress. "That is so odd," he exclaimed, but then he blinked and went on. "About your story, I think I missed a part, for I truly don't understand one thing. Why did the witch curse you?"

"Don't witches just like to do that kind of thing?" Dmitri asked, elbows framing

Efrosin's face, and his hands buried in Efrosin's fine hair. He twisted a longer piece of it around his finger. "If she had a reason, it is lost to me."

"It is rather amusing, I'm sure," Efrosin agreed. "Why, if I could curse people, I'd have so much fun. It's probably a very good thing that I cannot, though I do derive a great deal of mirth from merely imagining it."

"I can see," Dmitri said drily, though Efrosin had such a beautiful smile that it gave Dmitri a thrill to see it so artlessly there upon his face. "And your own affliction?"

"Oh yes, I am roundly cursed," Efrosin said. "As you yourself saw. I cannot walk, or crawl, or set my foot alight upon the ground without the effort of others."

"Have you tried pockets full of stones?"

"Of course. What do you take me for? A fool? Even if I am, my father is the king of this land, and he has physicians of the highest intellect at his command."

"The stones didn't work?"

"For a few moments, yes, long enough to walk perhaps ten steps, but then they become as part of me, and no longer hold me fast. They tried everything—diamonds in the soles of my shoes, gold in the hems of my clothing. All the heaviest gems were tried—zircon, sapphire, garnet, topaz, peridot—and not a one would weigh me down. Tying me often does the trick, but I must be fastened to something quite big. Bigger than me, and too heavy for me to carry."

"Hmm. You are surprisingly strong. I can attest to that." Dmitri caressed Efrosin's firm chest.

Efrosin grinned. "Yes. I prefer to be tied to someone, or many someones, because then they can ferry me about, which is a great deal more entertaining than being tied to a tree or a stone or a bed." His eyes lit up. "Though being tied here to your bed would be very fun indeed."

Dmitri couldn't disagree, and he felt his

prick react to the hint. He kissed the side of Efrosin's face, right where his lower lip met his cheek, and sighed. "Do you believe the rescue party will be here soon?"

"I hope not." Efrosin laughed. "I hope they do not find me for days and days."

Dmitri couldn't help feeling much the same. There were many things his body craved to do with Efrosin, many needs he was driven to meet. Efrosin was by far the most interesting person Dmitri had met in all his years, though granted, Dmitri had met only the odd trader or traveler. Even if Efrosin was strange, lighthearted and altogether too airy for his own good, he was a revelation.

"The physicians your father employed— what did they deduce your ailment to be?"

Efrosin laughed. "A curse, silly. My friend, perhaps you are the fool and not me." Joy flickered across his face. "Oh! Are you indeed my friend? Perhaps we have found our first true friend in each other."

Dmitri found himself smiling broadly,

his chest suffused with warmth. "Yes. I should like to call you my friend."

"Then I decree it so. How wonderful!" His forehead creased momentarily. "What were we talking about? Oh yes, I'm cursed, you ninny."

"Yes, but a curse is merely physics, is it not? For every curse, there must be an equal and opposite cure. Have you tried eating dirt? Perhaps a bit of good earth in your diet—"

"Enough," Efrosin said, putting up his hand. "Discussion of my predicament is so tiring. Have you tried a cure? What, pray tell, is the equal and opposite cure of your curse? Flight? Height?"

"Death," Dmitri said. "It is the only release from the bonds of this world."

Efrosin's eyes went wide. "Oh. Well then, let's not talk of that. I rather like you alive and touching me."

Dmitri ran his hands down Efrosin's body, and then beneath him to grip his buttocks, squeezing them as he pressed down with his hips, seeking evidence of Efrosin's renewed arousal. Efrosin's breath caught. "Ah, yes please. Do that again." Dmitri did as he was asked, and Efrosin crooned, his prick growing hard between them.

"Efrosin," Dmitri whispered. "Surely we should leave a signal, some sort of sign for the knights who are seeking you. I fear that they may ride on by."

"God willing," Efrosin said, his eyelashes fluttering on his cheeks. "Please, Dmitri, if you cannot go with me, then let me stay—at least until you bore me, which will likely happen soon. I am quite easily bored."

Dmitri felt he should be offended, but he was not. The idea that Efrosin would not wish to leave as soon as possible invigorated him, and he was deeply grateful for this short reprieve from loneliness. The last person he'd met had been an old trader, little more than skin and bones. He'd offered Dmitri some dried fruit, desperate for any meat. Dmitri had given him far more than he should have for the paltry berries, but the man's need had been great.

"And what should I do if I did not want you here?" Dmitri asked. "Toss you to the winds and hope they blew you home?"

Efrosin chuckled. "It would be much kinder of you to drop me in the river and let me swim for it. The river would never let me drown."

"I would never let you drown either, nor float away—"

"Nor leave this bed?" Efrosin asked, pulling Dmitri down for a kiss.

Dmitri had to admit that Efrosin's suggestion was tempting, especially as Efrosin whispered in his ear about the filthy, perverted things he'd seen the knights do, and suggested Dmitri try them out on him. To properly explore each one could take days, weeks, months, years.

Dmitri knew that he was a fool, but the seed Efrosin had planted in his heart cracked open, and the smallest of fragile shoots bloomed.

Chapter Five

"THIS ALE IS quite pleasing." Efrosin licked his lips before taking another bite of rabbit stew. "I've never tasted anything this good in the tavern near the castle. Of course my father forbade them to serve me ale, so I suppose it stands to reason. But now I'm of age—it's my birthday, did I mention?—and shall drink ale to my heart's content."

After another round of lovemaking, this time with their mouths to give Efrosin's tender ass a rest, they sat at the rough wooden table in their trousers. Well, Dmitri sat; Efrosin was tied to the bench, and his buttocks floated several inches above it, but at least he was able to reach the stew without spilling much.

Dmitri chuckled. "And what else does your heart desire on your special day?"

"Only one thing. To dive into a bracing body of water. That's what I want next, Dmitri." He felt his rump touch the board of the bench for a moment, and then he rose up again. So very curious.

Dmitri crunched on a biscuit—from a batch that wasn't light and flaky at all—but Efrosin got distracted by the delicious stew and strong ale before he could complain. "If you want to clean up, the water from the bowl is good enough for me, but I shall happily get out the tub and warm the water over the fire for you."

"A tub? As if that could replace the marvelousness of an open lake, surrounded by earth and sky. I should think the water in a tub would not even have the weight to hold me down."

"Have you never bathed in a tub before?" Dmitri asked.

In fact, Efrosin had not, at least not in his memory. For as long as he could recall, he'd spent more time in the river than out of it, and never needed to wash himself in a tub.

Besides, Efrosin wasn't interested in cleaning up. He wanted to swim, and he wanted to swim immediately, and he said as much.

"It's late in the day and far too cold to swim, Efrosin. Besides, it's not yet summer. The blossoms haven't even begun to fall from the branches of the Springsimmon."

"Oh the curse of the Springsimmon. Swim too soon and you'll die. I swim as soon as they can break the ice on the river and have done every year since I was a child." Dmitri looked pinched about the mouth in a way that Efrosin didn't quite like, and so he kissed the expression away.

Breaking off the kiss just as Dmitri moaned and leaned into it, Efrosin looked up from under his lashes and pressed his upper teeth into his lower lip. "I have heard that I am unbearably beautiful when wet. Not to mention I have it on the highest authority that I'm much easier to converse with when submerged; I have a bit of weight then. It is when I am most truly happy."

Dmitri softened. "I only want to keep you safe. But if you feel you must…"

"Yes, you must take me to the lake, or I will die of unhappiness." He unknotted the rope binding him to the table with a dramatic flourish and snatched up his white silk top before floating to the ceiling.

Efrosin knew that was an exaggeration while simultaneously feeling quite sure that it was absolutely true—should Dmitri fail to take him to the water, he would somehow dry up instantly and turn into dust. He'd been so happy only moments before, full of a physical, humming satisfaction, but now he felt a high-flying anxiety that would only dissipate once his body was enveloped in a watery embrace.

"But getting you there." Dmitri pulled on his shirt, regarding Efrosin with wide-eyed worry.

Efrosin flapped his hand to dismiss those charmingly realistic concerns as he slipped his arms into the silk. "You can strap me to your chest and carry me to the lake. You have rope and lengths of fabric. The knights do it all the time—especially Sir Carlisle. You are as strong and brave as a knight, are you not?"

He kicked off the ceiling and somersaulted through the air before noticing Dmitri's dark expression at the mention of Sir Carlisle. He wondered at the wild joy that stirred in him as he fanned the sparks of Dmitri's jealousy. "Though you don't have a beard like Sir Carlisle, so perhaps that makes all the difference."

Dmitri growled, snatched Efrosin by the ankle and dragged him down. He bound Efrosin to his chest with several long, rough ropes, and carried him out into the forest.

The sun still shone beyond the canopy of the trees, and Efrosin gazed up happily as Dmitri bore him away, arms tight around him.

The trees were so thick and grew so close to the water's edge that Efrosin barely had time to gasp before they were there. Ringed by trees, the lake sparkled in the late-day sun, a crystal blue that Efrosin thought he could get lost in forever. It was so much bigger than the river he was used to—he could barely make out the other side.

"Quick. Untie me." His palms itched, body twitching with the need to dive into the cool depths.

Dmitri obliged immediately, releasing the bonds and pushing Efrosin down gently to the water. Efrosin dove under and pulled off his silky clothing. He blew out, chuckling in his throat as bubbles gently tickled his face on their effervescent journey up. Following them, he broke through the shimmering surface, gasping for air, and shook the water from his eyes. He tossed his sodden garments to shore and grinned at Dmitri, who watched from the bank, a small smile playing at his lips.

After diving up, down and all around, exploring the depths of the lake, the water soothing on his naked skin, Efrosin flipped onto his back. He gazed up at the lovely sky—the very one that had almost swallowed him forever mere hours ago. How things had changed since then. How wondrous and strange.

Now the light faded around them, a rosy glow in the west indicating that the sun was on its way to bed. Efrosin twisted in the water, facing Dmitri again, admiring him where he sat amidst the new green grass shooting up all over the muddy bank. With his shirt tossed aside, exposing his hard stomach and handsome chest, and with his brown, steady eyes never leaving Efrosin for even a moment, Dmitri began to talk. "You know my story, so now I'll ask you. Why are you cursed? Let me guess—your father forgot to invite a powerful witch to your christening?"

Efrosin lifted an eyebrow and clucked his tongue. "Not every curse begins with a christening, my dear Dmitri." He pushed a bit harder with his legs to stay afloat.

"Of course not. Mine didn't. But yours did."

"Why, then you know the story already."

"Perhaps. There is much lacking in the gossip of old women trading their wares. So did a missed invitation cause the trouble?"

"Oh rather the contrary," Efrosin said, splashing lightly. "It could be argued that I'm cursed because Papa invited a powerful witch to my christening. Perhaps if she hadn't been invited, then she'd have just stayed away and minded her own affairs."

"Doubtful," Dmitri said, shrugging and leaning back against the embankment, his eyes straying up to the sky, clearly taking measure of the light. "Cursing is what witches like best. So…your father invited a powerful witch to your christening and then what?"

"Well, he invited two powerful witches, which is why I'm still here at all. Oh bother. Where to begin?" Efrosin chewed on his lower lip as he paddled languidly. "There is much to tell, but night is falling and I would dearly love it if you'd bugger me again before bedtime. Let me make small bones of this giant beast."

"As you wish," Dmitri chuckled.

"My mother, Queen Inna, died giving birth to me. After a suitable amount of time—one year to be precise—my father invited everyone of any importance to my combined birthday party and christening."

"Always ominous," Dmitri said.

"Indeed. My father invited Mother's eldest sister, Ereshkigal, the witch of the earth. She arrived and offered herself to my father as his new wife. She had loved him madly for years, you see, and never forgiven my mother for marrying him. My father laughed at her. As did I, though I was just a baby, and let's face it, I laugh at everything. She was insulted, of course, and gave me the delightful christening gift of this lovely curse in order to punish my father and to spite me for simply existing."

"But there was another powerful witch there?"

"Yes, my mother's younger sister, Uriti, the witch of fire. She wove a spell that tempered my curse with my mother's gift."

"Your mother's gift? I don't understand."

"My mother was the witch of strong waters. The only place I have any weight is in water from the river bearing her name." Efrosin indicated the lake of fresh, clear water he was swimming in. "The Inna River—and all of its lakes, streams, pools and ponds—is my favorite place to be. I would live in these waters if I could. All in all, it's not so bad of a curse. It could be much worse."

"Not so bad? If you say so."

"I met you because of the curse, didn't I?

Admit it, there is something delightful in that." Efrosin reached toward him and waggled his fingers, calling, "Come. Come in with me."

Dmitri shifted. "It is too early in the season to swim. Perhaps you're unaffected thanks to your affliction."

"Don't tell me you're truly afraid to swim before the Springsimmon blossoms fall. Do you always follow the rules?" Efrosin asked, sighing. "They make life so boring."

"Always follow the rules? I should say not. I took you home, didn't I? I kissed you and touched you, I bit your neck and pushed my prick into you, when any sensible person would have refused and found a way to summon the search parties instead. So no, clearly it is not required that I follow the rules. I have catered to your every need."

Efrosin chuckled. Rather than looking pleased or proud, Dmitri appeared a bit uncomfortable and puzzled over his choice to lie with Efrosin instead of follow his common sense. "Damn the Springsimmon then," Efrosin said, and splashed the water in a large arc that missed Dmitri only because he managed to roll quickly away. "Get in the water."

"No," Dmitri said, laughing. He dug in the sack he'd taken with them and tossed a bar of brown soap at Efrosin. It plopped into the water and popped up to the surface again. "Wash yourself. I want to get you back inside where you're safe." Dmitri's eyes glowed more brightly than the sun sinking closer to the trees. "And I want to lick and kiss your hole before I hold you down to fuck you again."

Efrosin licked his lips, remembering Dmitri's thick prick ramming into his ass, and the sudden descent of an ecstasy so arresting that he'd bitten down hard on the curve of Dmitri's shoulder. He now felt a sharp jolt in his gut at the sight of the reddish bruise left by his teeth and the purple blooms of love bites he'd sucked into Dmitri's chest and neck. He shivered.

"Tell me you don't want that too," Dmitri said, voice low. "You need it. We both do."

By all rights, Efrosin should be sated—his body still hummed pleasantly from their exertions, and his hole felt a bit sore and abused. Yet he already wanted it again. But he wanted it his way.

"It's true," Efrosin agreed, and smiled at Dmitri's triumphant expression. "But we have time. The night is almost upon us and they won't search for me in the dark. We'll have hours in your bed."

Dmitri cocked his head. "You sound almost…reasonable. It's odd. Nor are you laughing yourself sick at every moment."

"It's the water. It changes me." He lifted his hands in the air, presenting himself for a moment, before ducking beneath the surface again, coming up grinning. "Do you like it?"

Dmitri seemed to consider the question seriously. "I do. But I liked you before too."

His brow furrowed. "It's the water?"

"It must be." Efrosin stretched out his hand. "Come on."

"But it's freezing."

"It's not so cold." Efrosin turned on his brightest smile, summoning his more common enthusiasm from where he could feel it waiting in his lungs, like a balloon ready to rise. "Do dive in. It's thrilling!"

"I've no doubt. I'm sure it will thrill me until my skin is quite blue."

"Charming! Then you'll look like a water pixie." Efrosin tipped his head back, observing the sky turning the color of the knight's bruises after a tournament. It was dusk and anything was possible. "I have always wondered what it must be like to cavort with pixies. To be whisked away to their parties, dancing and twirling the night away, while godly men and women sleep unknowingly in their beds."

"Shh." Dmitri glanced around. "Don't speak of the blue folk. They're dangerous and should be respected."

Efrosin smiled, swallowed back a laugh—so much easier to do in the water—and took the advantage Dmitri had unwittingly offered. "If you get in, I won't mention the pixies again."

"And if I don't?"

Efrosin felt a surge of wicked delight. "Then I shall summon them."

As he opened his mouth to do just that, Dmitri put out his hand to stop him. "Please, Efrosin. Don't. My mother always warned me to stay far away from the earth fairies and water pixies. They are a menace."

Efrosin cleared his throat and projected his voice. "Blue pixies of—" He got nothing more out before he was swamped by a huge wave of water. Sputtering and wiping the excess from his face, he laughed and splashed back, amazed. Dmitri had leapt into the lake, breeches and all.

Together they were gleeful and happy, as the light faded around them and a rousing swirl of belching frogs lifted up their nightly song. The world was nothing but laughter and water, and slick skin against skin. Not to mention wet cloth that rubbed roughly against Efrosin's cock as he and Dmitri wrestled in the lake. They shoved and dunked each other, and Efrosin shocked Dmitri at one point by getting his footing in a shallow area, lifting Dmitri up out of the water and tossing him several feet despite the difference in their size.

"The water gifts you with inhuman strength too?" Dmitri chortled, splashing Efrosin's face and laughing when Efrosin choked, diving toward Dmitri and dunking him under.

"No," Efrosin said. "I'm simply much more than you think."

"I think you're everything," Dmitri exclaimed, which earned him a kiss, and then a push back into the water.

As the night closed around them, they tussled and raced, until finally Efrosin held

Dmitri's slick shoulder with one arm, chest to chest, his other hand twined with one of Dmitri's. His feet pressed into Dmitri's solid form, kicking at him playfully until suddenly Dmitri pulled his hand free from their clutch, reached between Efrosin's kicking legs and took hold of Efrosin's bollocks.

EFROSIN WENT COMPLETELY still, a sweet wonder engulfing him as Dmitri squeezed gently. Dmitri rolled them in his hand before gripping them a bit harder and Efrosin gasped. The water lapped at their skin, and the song of nightingales broke the quiet descending darkness as Efrosin let his legs relax in the water. Holding onto Dmitri's neck and breathing his breath, he stared into Dmitri's dark, warm eyes. *This is intimacy. This is trust. This is real.*

Efrosin had learned the rules of these

games from the best tutors his father could buy, but it was only now, his most sensitive part held firmly in Dmitri's grasp, that he understood the reason for them. And with a moan he realized that the deep place inside him, the one he'd only just unearthed in Dmitri's bed, was ever so much darker, deeper and full of secrets than he'd ever been able to imagine before.

"I don't want you to leave," Dmitri said, his voice rough.

Efrosin understood. Should the search parties find him, he would go. As wonderful as it was to dream of staying, he was a prince, and Dmitri was a woodsman cursed to remain on his land. They were not two of a kind, no matter how their bodies sang for each other now. The day would come—likely tomorrow—when Efrosin would be discovered, and he'd be carried away on horseback, strapped helplessly to Sir Carlisle's chest. Efrosin felt as though he'd swallowed a rock.

Dmitri massaged Efrosin's bollocks enough to knock them together inside the sac. Efrosin groaned as violent jolts of sensation shot through him, tightening his nipples and making his asshole clench desperately. Dmitri didn't seem to expect Efrosin to say anything, which was good, because all that Efrosin could do was feel— the vulnerability of his tender sac in Dmitri's calloused palm, the sweet pulse of his cock as the water swirled around it, and the pounding of his heart in his chest.

And just like that the newly found, heavy place inside him broke open and spilled out until he wasn't light like air and he wasn't wet like water. Instead he was dense like sun-warmed earth mixed into mud. He had never felt so thick, waiting with his lips resting against the stubble on Dmitri's chin, aching to be molded into shape.

Dmitri released Efrosin's sac and grabbed his cock instead, pulling it in a fast, eager rhythm. Efrosin moved, grabbing handfuls of

Dmitri's dark hair, finally kissing his lips. He licked into his open mouth, tasting water and spit, seeking the traces of his own seed that he'd shot so eagerly onto Dmitri's tongue in the cabin. And when he found it, he moaned, sang out in happiness and began to beg—for what he didn't know, just something more and something now.

Dmitri shook in Efrosin's arms and seemed to read his mind. "Yes, yes. I'll give it to you." They thrust against each other, legs tangling, until they slipped beneath the water, still kissing, and then pushed up and out again, coughing, gasping for breath and still unwilling to release the other's mouth.

The water and Dmitri's saliva mixed on Efrosin's tongue, a sweet elixir that he swallowed greedily as he struggled to keep afloat, until finally he pulled Dmitri by the hand toward the shallows by the bank. As they got close, he let go and flung himself onto all fours. Efrosin crawled forward as far as he dared, his hands and knees sinking into the mossy, murky bottom of the lake.

The water was up to his elbows and thighs, rooting him in wetness like a flower in the ground. Efrosin lifted his bare ass up in the air, arching like a dog in heat, begging to be mounted. The head of his hard cock breached the water, and he felt the constant soft movement around it, and the occasional brush of a fish. He dug his fingers farther into the sediment. His hole felt bruised and tender from their earlier endeavors, but he didn't care. Dmitri had unearthed the hot, desperate depths of him, and Efrosin couldn't get enough.

He panted, looking over his shoulder as Dmitri swam the short distance to him before shakily kneeling behind him in the shallow water. The very last of the sunlight illuminated him from behind, water dripping from his hair, nose and chin, his breeches plastered to him and streaked dark where Efrosin's feet had rubbed lake-bottom mud onto them in their tussle.

Dmitri's voice was rough. "Yes. God yes. You're so very beautiful, Efrosin. I will taste you and give you what you need." He didn't hesitate, grabbing Efrosin's buttocks and squeezing before spreading him apart. "It seems to wink at me," Dmitri marveled. "Let me kiss it, lick it."

"Please," Efrosin whimpered.

Efrosin shuddered and moaned, arching his ass toward Dmitri's mouth. He could feel the heat of Dmitri's breath on his hole, and his throat went dry. He bent his head to let his forehead drop into water. The wet, slopping sounds of the waves lapping at the shore came to his ears as he waited, pulse pounding for whatever was about to come.

He never had much patience out of the water, but now, fingers digging into soft, wet earth and Dmitri's taste on his tongue, he felt that every moment was worth waiting for, though he quaked with desire and shivered eagerly.

The first touch of Dmitri's mouth on

Efrosin's hole sent him scrambling and splashing in ecstatic shock, and Dmitri grabbed hold of his hips to haul him close. "It tickles!" Efrosin gasped, shoving his ass back for more. He squirmed, laughing deep in his belly as Dmitri swirled his tongue all around Efrosin's asshole.

"It tickles, Dmitri."

As soon as he said the name, he felt a sensation almost like a blanket covering him. Then the tickle was no longer funny at all, but so deliriously good that Efrosin forgot he was in the water, collapsing down farther and farther, shoving his ass higher up, grinding it against Dmitri's mouth, teeth and chin. He suddenly found himself coughing and choking, having dropped his face into the lake in his ecstasy.

Dmitri held his hips tightly and didn't stop until he finally groaned and flung himself on top of Efrosin, rubbing his cock between Efrosin's buttocks. He wrapped his arms around Efrosin and clung tight, all of his weight bearing down on Efrosin's knees and hands, which sunk deeper into the muck.

"Please," Efrosin begged, and he realized he'd said it so many times now, it was a litany, a chant, and it had lost all meaning until he added, "Fuck me."

Dmitri pulled back enough to get his hand between them, and Efosin yelled at the thick intrusion as Dmitri pushed his cock head against Efrosin's tender asshole, and then Efrosin's skin prickled with encompassing pleasure as Dmitri breached the muscle, sliding inside—steady, heavy, and filling him with weight.

Dmitri's long, strong fingers gripped Efrosin's cock, and together they rocked and moaned in the mud at the edge of the lake, the water splashing against their thighs. When Efrosin's wrists gave out and he fell down to his elbows, it splashed them in the face as they hunched and writhed together.

Dmitri's teeth raked over Efrosin's shoulder then latched onto the back of his neck, worrying there as he rammed his cock into Efrosin. Then, like an escaped prayer, Efrosin cried out, his body tensing as he reached into the surprisingly deep well of feeling inside him, grabbing fistfuls of wet dirt as he did.

Time stopped, shot through with rapture, until Efrosin burst out of the depths and back up to the edges of his skin, bringing it all with him. Wild cries and convulsions rattled him as he shot his seed into the water that had always been home.

Gasping and exhausted, Efrosin could barely keep his face above the surface while Dmitri moved inside him with slamming, long strokes. He reached back to grab Dmitri's hip and clutch him close when Dmitri cried out against his back, and hot, heavy bursts of his pleasure filled Efrosin's ass.

"Don't go," Dmitri whispered.

Efrosin opened his mouth to say the things he knew he'd say at any other time.

Easy things. Hurtful things. The kinds of things that had tripped off his tongue since he'd uttered his first words.

But there in the shallows as the stars twinkled into sight, the heavy warmth of Dmitri's body covering his, and with Dmitri's spendings weighing inside him, he stayed silent instead.

$$Chapter\ Six$$

AFTER THEY'D TRYSTED, they had both been covered in so much mud that they'd had to dive back into the deeper parts of the lake with Dmitri's soap to scrub themselves clean. Then Dmitri had strapped Efrosin to his chest again—this time naked as night was black, unwilling to risk him getting caught on a breeze as he put his clothes on.

He'd carried him back through the thick forest, walking slowly in the dark so as not to trip over downed limbs or undergrowth. All the while, Efrosin tormented him by pressing kisses onto the crook of his neck, licking the shell of his ear and sucking maddeningly on his earlobe. By the time they reached the cabin, both of their pricks were aching, and Dmitri had wasted no time tying Efrosin to the bed and buggering him again until, exhausted, they'd finally slept.

At dawn, Dmitri listened to the sounds of the cabin creaking, and the crackle of the dying embers in the fireplace. He watched Efrosin sleep in the trappings of the covers Dmitri had rigged to keep him against the mattress, additionally secured by the weight of Dmitri's leg tossed over Efrosin's body.

Efrosin's eyelashes lay against his cheek, and his mouth was slightly open, red-lipped from such quantities of kissing and biting, as well as the exertion of sucking Dmitri's prick. A pleasant expression danced on Efrosin's face, as though he was dreaming about something vaguely amusing. Dmitri touched his finger to the corner of Efrosin's up-turned mouth and decided that, knowing Efrosin, he probably was.

Dmitri remembered Efrosin's words the

night before. "Is it always this way, Dmitri?" Efrosin had asked. "I'm so happy. I don't think I've ever been quite this happy. I've been delighted and cheerful and eager and silly and many other things, but this is a different thing altogether. I feel quite full with it."

Looking at Efrosin, so effortlessly handsome in his sleep, Dmitri felt full with it too. But then he frowned as the heaviness of reality settled over him. This couldn't last for long, and that it might in fact end this very day filled him with a sense of wounded despair. Yet what was best for Efrosin had to come before his own petty needs and wants.

Sighing, Dmitri carefully rose and pulled on his warm breeches, dried by the fire the night before. As he slipped on his rough shirt, so much less fine than Efrosin's soft clothes, he glanced at the bed. Efrosin snuffled softly but didn't wake. Dmitri looked closer, and he blinked a bit in surprise. Efrosin's head, hands and legs were touching the mattress. They did not float as they had the morning before, and as Dmitri watched, one of Efrosin's feet slipped from the bed and dangled close to the ground instead of drifting into the air.

As Dmitri stared, Efrosin's foot began to slowly rise, as though regaining its levity, and soon it was floating again. Dmitri frowned, then shrugged as he took up the sharp blade he kept for shaving as he usually did in the mornings. But then, remembering Efrosin's numerous mentions of Sir Carlisle's beard, he left it.

Dmitri tugged his boots into place and quickly shoved his hunting knife, some rope and a biscuit into his bag, deciding to check the traps. He'd never made it the day before, and he did not like to think of an injured animal left suffering in his traps for lack of a human hand to bring it the comfort of death.

Dmitri hovered by the bed, his hand outstretched to shake Efrosin awake, but at the last moment he refrained, not wanting to disturb Efrosin's rest after their long night of intense lovemaking. He needed to rest, possibly to heal, after the rough coupling they'd done in the small hours of the morning. Dmitri's heart felt pricked as he observed the tousled golden hair against Efrosin's forehead, and the thud of Efrosin's pulse in his neck. Even it looked light and cheerful, beating away there like the flutter of a bird's wings.

He pressed a kiss to Efrosin's lips and soothed him back to deep sleep with a soft "Shhh," and then went on his way.

He hadn't gone very far into the woods when a black bird swooped onto his path, cawing. Dmitri stepped back, a little frightened by the way the bird snapped its wings and blocked his way. It was then that he felt her, the great, terrible weight of presence behind him. He turned slowly away from the bird, reluctant to take his eyes from it lest it attack, but needing to see what creature had appeared at his back all the same.

The old woman was small and not small all at once. Her hair was coated with mud, and tiny seedlings grew from her head—evergreens and maples, tiny oaks and baby lindens. Her hands and feet were thick with dirt, almost as if she'd used them to claw out of the earth, and her dress looked made of black moss, with ants and small beetles crawling over it. Her face was startling to look upon, so dirty and streaked with grime, but her eyes glittered provocatively, and her lips curled in a withering smile. Dmitri stared.

"Don't you have a kiss for your mother?" she asked, leaning toward him with her mud-smeared lips puckered.

He pulled back instinctively to get away from the fetid smell of her breath and person. "You're not my mother. You're the witch who cursed me as a babe."

She cackled. "I'm everyone's mother, and no one's mother, boy." Her fingers curled into claws and she lurched at him, grabbing a fistful of his shirt. "If not for me, you'd all be dead—especially you—and yet do any of you want to kiss the old woman, fill her with your sweet young prick?" She spat on the ground.

Dmitri's throat felt dry as he swallowed convulsively. The woman—no, the witch—ran one finger down the side of his cheek and trailed it over his lips. "All red and swollen, I see," she said. "With the telltale signs of a man's stubble against your chin." Her finger was bone dry as it touched the tender skin of his jaw, raw from Efrosin's evening beard. "Cavorting with a missing prince perhaps?"

Dmitri's tongue felt heavy, as if weighted by magic, and he could only stare at the woman as she nodded slowly and licked her lips with a tongue that was dark as the most fertile soil. "Oh yes, the entire kingdom is looking for him. It seems he floated away." She tsked slowly. "Such a shame. His father fears he's dead."

Dmitri felt stabbed through with guilt.

He hated the thought that anyone might feel the same grief that he endured after his parents' death. He should have tried harder to get Efrosin back home or to draw attention to his whereabouts. But Efrosin had such need—desires echoed in Dmitri's own heart.

"The king's mourning is full of rage. He holds the prince's minder responsible, even as the man scours the land for his missing charge. The king will execute the man's wife and children at dawn should the prince not be returned. The king is an unreasonable man—so cruel, so selfish. I understand him. I'm cruel and selfish too."

Dmitri shuddered. "I must get Efrosin back to the castle. He said he could swim…"

Her eyes flashed and her long nails dug into Dmitri's chest. "Oh yes, he can swim. But don't fret, his saviors are on their way. My friend here," she indicated the bird, "told the young prince's manservant where they could find him. How long will it be, darling, before they arrive?"

The bird cawed.

"Ah, within the hour," the witch said.

Dmitri's emotions swelled inside him, a jumble of relief that Efrosin would be safe, despair at losing him, and violent terror of the witch and her bird. He opened his mouth to speak but could not. The witch raised her other hand and held it to Dmitri's heart. His eyes bulged and he began to shake; his heart felt as if it was slowing down and growing rigid in his chest.

He could not break his gaze from the witch's face. He tried to force his legs to move, to run, but he was held fast to the ground as though he'd been turned to stone. The witch kissed him, shoving her tongue into his mouth, and he gagged at the taste of mud and rotting compost.

She grimaced when she pulled back and said, "Disgusting. You're corrupted by love." Then suddenly Dmitri's knees buckled and he was on the ground at her feet. She pointed at him. "Stay."

He found that he could not move even if he wanted to. He could not even blink.

"Let me tell you a story, little one," the old woman said, her teeth shining in the morning light like beads of black onyx. "It's a very important story, you see. It contains your life and death. So pay attention."

And then the witch told Dmitri her tale—and his.

ONCE UPON A time, there was a strong-running river called Inna, named for the beautiful witch of the waters. She was one of four beautiful sisters, each a sorceress, and each holding dominion over an element.

The first born was Ereshkigal, witch of earth. She was dark and thick of body, with skin that was milky-white and eyes that were the color of fresh dung. She was born old, older than time, and strong. Many common humans believed her to be a steady sort, earthy and rich with generosity. But she shifted violently beneath the surface, full of hot, liquid yearning that boiled and bubbled, passionate and wanting.

The second born was Aira, witch of the wind. She was beautiful with her white hair, soft as clouds, and her blue eyes as vast as the sky. But she was a flighty, reckless thing, never staying any place for long, darting from lover to lover, changeable as the wind can be, incapable of attachment or loyalty.

The third born was Uriti, witch of fire. She too was beautiful, with red and blue-streaked hair, bright cheeks and flaming eyes. But she was hot tempered and hard to control, often leaping from bed to bed, burning a path of intense but short-lived passion through the world, destroying many a marriage and home as she went.

The fourth born was Inna, witch of waters. She was beautiful with light hair and eyes that sparkled like the sun dancing on waves. Her manner was easy and accommodating, flowing from one activity to the next, easily bypassing obstacles and laughing beautifully along the way. Her embrace was complete, and many a man drowned in love for her.

Then King Leo rode into their lives.

He arrived in the valley where the known world converges on the unknown on horseback, bathed in blood from battle, adorned in armor, shining like the sun. The sisters waited there for him, having all four felt the pull of destiny; all together in the same place for the first time in their lives.

Leo was strong of arm and stronger of mind, unyielding in his intentions. He announced his desire to wed one of them, and commanded each to give their best argument why she, and only she, should be his wife.

Aira laughed and departed at once, preferring the joy of airy freedom. Uriti raged briefly at his impudence, scorched his armor and then disappeared as well, eager to get back to the bed she had been burning with lust when she'd received the summons.

Inna, for her part, merely waited to see what would happen next, good-naturedly dancing about, her hair flowing out behind her, and her feet tripping easily over the rocks and fallen trees.

As for Ereshkigal, she fell in love with him upon first sight.

The truth of Ereshkigal is that she is not steady. She is cruel, changeable and punishing. Rivers of lava from an erupting volcano are her temper tantrums. The violent lurching of the ground splitting apart, and coming together, destroying everything that has been built on top of the earth are her rages. Winters of starvation after crops fail are her most even-handed punishment. Ereshkigal merely laughs and shrugs as mothers and children waste away, crying out in hunger, and begging, "Why?"

The answer, dear child, to that time-old question is this—she despises you for raking the skin of her beloved earth with the tines of your plows, for scarring her, for taking the fruits of her land to multiply and grow your own kind, and not one of you making love to her, stuffing your prick into her old, worn carcass with glee and joy, nor caring if she herself is barren and lonely, not noticing that no one loves her gently, or takes her roughly, or fills her with sweet progeny of her own.

Selfish, all of you, wanting only what you can have. Wheat and fruit for yourselves, and grass for your horses, scorning the old lady who is too proud to beg for the sweet taste of love. Scorned and laughed at, despised and rejected by men and women alike. Men like Leo, who spit on Ereshkigal despite her love for him.

"Get thee away from me, wretched old cow with the teeth of rotting corpses," Leo cried, shoving Ereshkigal aside and setting his eyes on Inna. "Why would I want an old woman like you when I can plow that sweetness there?"

Ereshkigal boiled, bubbled and raged. For Ereshkigal was the one who was fertile, the one who should be plowed and sown. That was what she was made for, could the fool not see? She was earth, she was mother, she was giving and cruel and harsh and generous. She was young and old. She was the beginning and the end.

Inna was beautiful but not meant to grow life in her belly, not meant to push that life out and live to do it again. But the king saw only her easy beauty, lusted for her, and wanted her for his own. Inna, for her part, felt the tug of destiny, if not the consuming fire of love, and turned her back on her powers to marry the king, abandoning witchhood to be the wife of King Leo. Death is what comes of a witch subverting her power for the love of a vain, violent king.

Ereshkigal saw it all. She saw the future and she knew her revenge would come. Her sister would die, and then Ereshkigal would destroy the king's happiness by cursing his murdering infant son. She made him repellent to the earth, certain that the sky and the stars would claim him 'ere long.

But even a witch like Ereshkigal cannot control it all. Her sister, Uriti, saved the child with his mother's gift of water, and within that wet embrace the curse does not hold dominion. Even now the thought makes Ereshkigal shriek with rage.

And then there is you, born Dmitri, the little farmer, born straight from the dirt of the earth—and fathered by the fairies. Oh yes, my boy. You think that fool woodcutter, old as he was, got your mother with child? Don't be stupid. His prick could barely piss much less crow with proud, life-giving seed.

Once upon a time, there was a lonely woodcutter's wife. Beautiful and young, married to a man who was good, indeed he was, but he was old and unable to rouse lust in one as ripe as she. The old man traveled often, carting his wood from house to house, selling it for pennies, while his wife was left alone to tend their garden and cabin.

One such day, the mud-baked earth fairies, those bound to the earth and tasked with making the land fertile, heard the keens of her loneliness and distress. They felt your mother's wish for a child, and could not bear to see her need go unfulfilled. They are empathetic creatures, earth fairies, obnoxiously eager to encourage life at all turns.

It can't be helped. Just as they are bound to the land, they are compelled to meet the needs of humans. So the fairies grew tall with their urge to comfort her, and when they were quite human height, they knocked on her cabin door. For hours they took turns with her.

Have no fear, boy. It was not rape. She sobbed only with pleasure and grateful joy at the unflagging thrusts of their robust pricks, just as you trembled with gratitude while you plowed the cursed prince you're harboring in your bed because you could not refuse his need.

And when the fae left your mother shivering in wanton delight, covered in their mud and filled with their spendings, they returned, right-sized, to her garden. It burst into full bloom and bulged with early ripened crops.

She was planted full of you, Dmitri, her little farmer. Full of earth and life, making you part mud, and far too much fairy. I sensed the wrong done, the earth fairies planting where they ought only to tend, but they have minds of their own, don't they? Do they obey Ereshkigal? No, they do not. But I had no need to curse you, boy. Your fairy half binds you to this land, alone for all your days.

Until you plucked the prince from the sky, seducing him into your arms, weighing him down, undermining my curse. You have seen the evidence yourself. Your presence gives him weight, your very name on his lips drags his toe against my sacred ground. Why do you think he was so taken with you? You fulfill his every need. Oh don't bother with your sob story of how you never meant to thwart me, that you didn't know, that you never dared. It is your destiny; you could not have prevented it if you tried.

Together, you and he are earth and air and water, and your passion is fire—a balance that offsets my curse. But I cannot allow it. Are you listening, child? This is where it gets interesting.

There behind you is a lake, or shall I say there was a lake? For within the hour it will be empty, disappeared through a tiny hole— just about the size of your big toe—flowing into an underground channel out and away to the ocean, hundreds of miles from this land. As it goes, so will every river, pond, lake, well and stream in the Kingdom Goldenthal, now and forever more. No rain will fill them, no snows will melt and make them replete again.

The people will thirst. They will suffer and die. It shan't take long—don't worry. It's an ugly death, but a fast one all the same. It takes longer for my bird here to peck one to death, and longer yet to starve. I could be less merciful, you see.

Why, you want to know? Because Leo's son, my sister's brat, will not have both love and water. My curse will not be undermined by your freakish existence. It is a correction I make to a wrong done—you should not exist, and your lover should not go unpunished for the sins of his father. I was merciful when you were a babe, allowing you to live, bound to the earth that is a part of you and your fairy fathers.

There will be no more mercy from Ereshkigal. My misery will belong to all.

How is it possible to dry up every last drop of water, you ask? A curse, of course. And just as you say, for every curse, there is a cure, if only one can find it. But I won't make you hunt. I'll tell you now how you may save your prince's happiness and the people's wretched lives.

Are you listening carefully? That small hole I punched in the earth under the lake is enchanted and can only be filled by the big toe of a man. This man must voluntarily give his life to plug the hole, and it will not stay sealed should his toe ever be removed. Clever, isn't it? For Ereshkigal has always been clever. One life sacrificed shall save so many.

And think, Dmitri, you will be free. Just as the fae who sired you are no longer bound to this earth now that they are but ashes on the wind, you'll be free. Did I mention the man who gallantly plugs this hole must be half-fairy, half-human and in love with a prince who lacks gravity? Do you know of any such person?

I think you might.

<h1 style="text-align:center">Chapter Seven</h1>

GEOFFRY TIED HIS naked charge securely to the bench next to the wooden table in the small cabin where they'd found him and began to clean Efrosin. The lad was covered in the remnants of intercourse, and any thought Geoffry might have had of Efrosin being unwillingly seduced was countered by his delighted recounting of far too many details of the events.

"It truly is the best feeling, is it not, Geoffry? I feel I've sorely missed out before now, and it's quite unfair to be deprived of so many years of pleasure."

"You are not so very old, sire," Geoffry

said, his face flaming bright red as he wiped at the dried evidence of Efrosin's enjoyment. "There are many years yet to experience this joy." He cleared his throat. "Sire, it is imperative that you dress. We must soon be on our way. There is a dire situation that can only be—"

Efrosin didn't appear to be listening. "His name is Dmitri, did I tell you? Oh you must meet him, Geoffry. He is so very funny."

"You think everyone is funny."

"But he truly is. He buried his parents! In graves he dug himself!"

Geoffry blinked, untied Efrosin from the bench and watched him bob directly up to the low ceiling. "Truly, we must go. As I told you earlier, I'm lucky to be alive. Your father nearly hanged me the first day, and my children—"

Efrosin clapped as his eyes lit up. Kicking off the ceiling, he grabbed hold of Geoffry's lapels, dangling there in front of him, his feet drifting heavenward. "Oh yes, bravo. Tell me, Geoffry, how did you do it? How did you survive such peril? It must have been so thrilling."

"I promised your father, should he spare my life, that I would bring you to him before sunrise tomorrow. He holds my dear ones in my stead, so I must get you back to the castle, sire."

Efrosin prattled on as if Geoffry hadn't spoken. "I'm glad, by the way, that you live. I had writ you off for dead. Even Dmitri will be surprised because I told him you had surely been put to death for losing me. You must meet him. His eyes are like chocolate, and his lips are sweeter than Papa's best wine, and he smells of the earth and tastes like dirt. Did you know that dirt tastes ever so delightful? Well, it does when it's Dmitri."

Geoffry cleared his throat, blushing as he said, "Surely there is someone who will taste just as fine at home."

"I think not. Of every man I know,

Dmitri is the only one I want. Well, except perhaps Sir Carlisle, but he does not dabble in men. Which is a shame, because his thighs and arms are so very strong, and—"

"Sire," Geoffry stopped him before he could go on. Sir Carlisle and the other knights of Efrosin's escort waited just outside the door, all of them embarrassed enough by the state in which they'd found his highness—tied to a bed with a rosy, hard prick, wet at the tip from longing, and clearly thoroughly debauched.

Geoffry put aside the uncomfortable memory and went back to attempting to engage Efrosin's cooperation. "Please put on your clothing."

Efrosin ignored him. "No, no, even though Sir Carlisle has many fine qualities, there is no one but Dmitri for me." He sighed, allowing Geoffry to help him with a shirt. "Can you not simply send a message? Surely the knights can ride on ahead, tell my father that I live, and I can stay with Dmitri.

I told you, I'm not ready to leave him yet."

"Your father will not believe us, Prince Efrosin. He's out of his mind with suspicion and grief. He'll think I am lying to buy my children time. And you will find someone more…suitable. At court. Where your father awaits you with a heavy heart, mourning you for dead."

"Oh poor Papa," Efrosin said airily, and Geoffry sighed. Some things never changed. He gathered more water on the rough cloth he'd found and scrubbed at the clumps of spendings in Efrosin's golden chest hair. Then again some things did.

"Wait—what was that you said about your children?" Efrosin asked.

Geoffry blinked in surprise. "We must return by dawn, or the king will see my offspring dead for my crime of losing you."

Efrosin frowned. "But that is quite un-fair, is it not?"

"It is, sire. So we must be going. We will return with hours to spare, but still, let us make haste."

"Indeed. We must just find my Dmitri and we may be off."

"The gentleman will not be going with us?" Geoffry asked.

"Of course not."

Geoffry was pleased that Efrosin now saw the folly of that association. "That is well."

"Dmitri is cursed to remain here on his land," Efrosin said. "Which is why I must say goodbye and let him know that I'll return to him anon."

Geoffry helped his prince get his stained pants on and quietly signaled for the knights. He hated to go against Efrosin's wishes, but he had no choice.

"Wait! What are you doing?" Efrosin asked, pushing against Sir Carlisle's shoulders as he was effortlessly plucked from the air and restrained.

"We don't have time," Geoffry said. "I'm sorry, but you must leave without saying goodbye."

Efrosin squirmed and kicked. "You said we have hours to spare."

Geoffry was appalled by the young man's lack of manners when he actually attempted to bite Sir Carlisle in his attempt to get free. Once they had wrapped him tightly, and Sir Carlisle exited the hovel, Efrosin stilled and grew quiet, likely due to his fear of the endless sky.

Geoffry felt unsettled as they climbed upon their horses with Sir Carlisle holding Efrosin tight to his chest while he mounted his great stallion. Geoffry could not take his eyes from Efrosin's pale face as they rode away, walking the horses in the close quarters of the thick, cloying forest. "Are you quite all right, sire? You look," and here Geoffry frowned, "sad."

"I find I am not at all right, actually," Efrosin answered, staring back the way they came. "Something is lodged inside my chest. I find it rather hard to breathe. I believe this horrible feeling would stop if I went back. I must be with Dmitri."

"You must continue home."

"But this feeling. This horrible, awful feeling, Geoffry." Efrosin's expression was stricken. "Is it gravity? It feels quite heavy and hard."

"No, sire, I believe this feeling is what we call 'love'. But knowing you as I do, I believe it will pass."

"No. Love is what I felt when I was happy in Dmitri's arms last night. This is something horrible and I don't think I can bear it much longer."

Sir Carlisle shifted Efrosin against his chest, a bewildered expression on his face as Efrosin's eyes took on an odd glow, and he began to chant in a whisper, "Dmitri, Dmitri, Dmitri, Dmitri," over and over with a backing note of determination in his voice that made Geoffry shiver.

Sir Carlisle grunted and hefted Efrosin a bit. "He grows heavy," he said. "What sort of magic is this? I have carried him since he was but a child, and he has never weighed an ounce."

Efrosin began to shout Dmitri's name, and as he did Sir Carlisle struggled with his sudden weight. Geoffry cried out as Efrosin's fingers worked quickly to untie his restraints, and when Sir Carlisle tried to grip him tighter, Efrosin threw a wild and direct punch, landing it squarely on Sir Carlisle's nose. Blood spurted, shouts erupted, and before Geoffry's stunned eyes, Efrosin jumped from the stallion's back and lighted upon the earth.

"Dmitri! Dmitri!" Efrosin's body rose lightly in the pause between the words, his feet barely touching the ground, but he did not float away. As the brave knights sat frozen and shocked upon their horses, Efrosin raced into the forest, stumbling over branches but never quite falling down, screaming his lover's name.

Geoffry's heart raced madly. His Efrosin, his prince, was cured! Joy rivaled with frustration at Efrosin's selfishness, and despair for the impending loss of Geoffry's family should Efrosin not return home by sunrise. He called out, "We must retrieve him!"

Their horses raced down the path into the deep of the woods, following the sound of Efrosin's voice on the wind.

EFROSIN'S THROAT FELT torn. His voice was fading fast. The force with which he had to yell Dmitri's name in order to stay on the ground was more than he could sustain for long. He didn't know what magic allowed for this miracle, but he'd felt the changes in him from the moment he met Dmitri and the first time he'd uttered his name.

"Dmitri! Dmitri!" If his voice gave way entirely, he would be lost. With that in mind, he headed toward the lake.

Just let the knights try to drag him from the water. He could out-swim them all. He was not leaving until he had seen Dmitri, pledged his love and given his promise to return. If Dmitri should return from wherever he had wandered and find the cabin empty, he would fear Efrosin had been caught on a breeze and floated away.

The thought of Dmitri frightened for his sake made Efrosin's skin feel tight and prickly, as if it did not quite fit right. He supposed the sensation was what Geoffry had told him was "empathy" or perhaps "guilt", but either way he didn't like it, and he would risk anything to stop Dmitri from feeling such pain.

Besides, he told himself, the castle was but a few leagues' ride away, and they had until sunrise to stay his father's hand. There was time yet.

As the lake came into view Efrosin's breath caught in his throat, and he lifted off the ground in his stunned silence. The water was low—quite low—little more than neck-deep in places where he and Dmitri had been in well over their heads only the night before. He floated another foot higher as he spied a person in the middle of the lake, standing stock still, the water coming up almost to the man's chin.

"Dmitri," he breathed. His toe grazed land. "Dmitri!"

Dmitri did not turn, his shoulders set squarely to the southern mountains. Efrosin chanted Dmitri's name, his toes barely touching the ground, and he dove into the shallow water without bothering to take off his clothes. He felt the sweet relief of the lake's embrace only dimly in his panic, for there was something wrong. He didn't know just what, but a strong physical pull in his gut, groin and chest told him to swim to Dmitri. Now.

As Efrosin approached, Dmitri's lips were set in a grim line, his eyes closed. When Efrosin called his name, he did not respond.

Efrosin's stomach twisted painfully, like the stomach cramps he had after eating bad oysters as a child, and he felt he might be sick though he didn't know quite why. Efrosin finally reached Dmitri and gripped his arms tightly, shaking him, expecting him to move easily through the water and slide wetly into his arms.

Instead, Dmitri held fast. Efrosin shook him, "Dmitri! Are you caught?"

"Efrosin..." Dmitri's eyes opened and his voice was soft. "Am I dead already? Are you my angel even still?"

"Dead? I should think not. I've found you now. Have no fear. I'll save you, Dmitri. Just hold on. We must act quickly. The water is rising fast—where did it disappear to?"

Dmitri stared at him tenderly. "How did you get here? Did you fly?"

"Are you ill? Answer me, Dmitri. Tell me where to pull!"

Dmitri's eyes sharpened then. He shook his head. "Leave me. It's too late."

Fear gripped Efrosin far beyond his prior imagining. He dove beneath the surface and, following the line of Dmitri's body down, he finally located the problem—the big toe of Dmitri's left foot was caught in a tight hole. Efrosin pulled hard at Dmitri's leg, but the toe was stuck fast, and Dmitri did naught to help.

Lungs burning, Efrosin burst through to the surface and saw even in that short amount of time the lake had risen to cover Dmitri's chin. From the corner of his eye he saw the knights and Geoffry dismount from their horses near the shore. They called for him, but he remained focused.

"You must help me, Dmitri. Pull as I tug. We must get you free. The water is rising."

"Efrosin," Dmitri said, reaching out to him, pulling him close. "Don't fight it. Only know that I did this for you and for the people of our land."

"Whatever are you talking about?"

Efrosin's throat was so tight he could barely speak.

"I don't have time to explain it." Even now the water was slipping into his mouth, and Dmitri had to tip his head back to keep it from filling his throat completely. "There's only one thing you have to know—my toe must never leave the hole at the bottom of the lake or the water will drain from the kingdom. No matter what happens, never dislodge it. Do I have your promise?"

Efrosin shook his head violently. "I will never leave you here."

"It's my dying wish." He coughed, choking on the relentless water. "You can't take my toe from its place in the bottom of the lake. Promise me now before I die."

Efrosin blinked rapidly and then gave a short, fast nod. He turned and yelled to the knights swimming toward them. "I need a knife! Bring me a knife!"

"It's too late," Dmitri said, gasping for breath. "I'll be free now. I know you can't mourn me, but do think of me from time to time." He spluttered and coughed desperately.

The water closed over his mouth, and then over his nose and eyes. Efrosin cried out in agony, tugging at Dmitri's shoulders as he stared down at his lover's brown eyes gazing up at him from beneath the clear water.

Then the bubbles of Dmitri's final breath released, and Efrosin dove beneath the water, pressing his lips to Dmitri's and breathing into his mouth. But Dmitri did not take the breath, and there beneath the water his body spasmed and jerked, his eyes going wide before he stilled completely.

Efrosin broke the surface, shouting again for a knife, and when the knights reached him he grabbed the blade from Sir Carlisle's hand and swam down to Dmitri's foot, slicing in rough, jagged swipes at his toe. The bone was hard to sever, but Efrosin's panic gave him strength. Blood clouded the water, rising and twisting around him as he worked, but he didn't give up until Dmitri's body was released.

All but for his toe, which Efrosin left as promised in the greedy hole at the bottom of the lake.

AT THE WATER'S edge, Efrosin knelt in the shallows and watched Geoffry work on Dmitri. A sound clawed its way from Efrosin's throat, piercing the air around them. He couldn't stop touching Dmitri, his fingers clinging to the wet fabric of his breeches.

Geoffry pounded on Dmitri's chest, slapped his face, lifted him up and thumped on his back. Still Dmitri's eyes that had been rich with life like the most fertile loam remained unseeing. Time seemed to stop. The knights stood watch, unmoving. The leaves on the trees were still; the very clouds in the sky were frozen. The only motion was Geoffry as he worked, and the treacherous lake as it deepened around Efrosin's thighs.

"I shall choke," Efrosin cried. "I am crushed beneath this weight. You must save him, Geoffry. You must!"

Geoffry worked tirelessly, but for naught. Finally, Efrosin felt his heart sink to the lowest depths of hell as Geoffry looked up at him with tired, sad eyes. "Sire, he is gone."

Efrosin could not breathe, could not feel his heart beat where it had plummeted so deep into despair. He threw himself up out of the water, onto Dmitri's body, gripping his neck tightly. "No!"

To the shock of everyone, Efrosin burst into sobs. What's more, he did not float at all. Like a cloud erupting with heavy rain, he found his gravity weeping against his dead lover's neck. He flowed with hot, wild tears that rushed from him in a mad torrent that could not be staved. They ran down his face, one after another, onto Dmitri's unmoving chest.

The world seemed to release its bated breath. The outcome had been determined. Dmitri, half fairy of the land, was dead. The wind tossed the leaves in the trees, and the clouds skittered across the sky. The knights fell to their knees in prayer, and Geoffry ran his fingers over Efrosin's hair, clucking a sound meant to soothe.

Efrosin pressed his lips against Dmitri's motionless mouth, sobbing into him, and as his tears fell into Dmitri's still-open eyes, he choked out, "Heaven can't be better than me, Dmitri. Please. I need you. Don't go."

I need you.

Don't go.

DMITRI HAD NEVER known such freedom. His soul was boundless, infinite. The light was bright and comforting as he traveled toward it effortlessly, and he was reminded of

Efrosin rising up toward the sky. The thought hurt and he grabbed his chest, glancing down to find he was rising above the earth.

Kneeling knights and a weary man circled his body, and upon his lifeless form was Efrosin—delightful, joyful, beautiful Efrosin—sobbing without restraint, his tears raining down on Dmitri's empty face.

He looked down into his own eyes, wet now with Efrosin's tears, and shivered. He wondered at Efrosin's grief. Did he…was this for him? He had not imagined Efrosin capable.

I need you.

Don't go.

It reached him like a prayer, a magic enchantment. Yet now that he was released from the mortal coil, his fairy blood no longer tugged at him to meet Efrosin's need. Now it was only Dmitri's own heart and soul that yearned to quench that desire, comfort that grief and fill Efrosin with an answering adoration. He glanced up one last time at the warm, golden light awaiting him. He turned away…

Heavy.

His lungs burned, a terrible pressure in his chest. Coughing, Dmitri jerked up, knocking Efrosin from him. He expelled lake water from his lungs until he vomited it in a massive stream. Hands beat against his back and shoulders, and he gasped for air, finally dragging in a long, clean breath. He became aware of a fiery sensation in his left foot, a throbbing agony he couldn't explain.

Efrosin still sobbed next to him. Dmitri tried to tell him he was back, and Efrosin could stop crying now, but nothing came out save a croak. Efrosin's hands were greedy on him, gripping his wet shirt, twisting into his short hair, and his mouth was everywhere, kissing his lake-water lips, eyelids, nose, neck, mouth, cheeks and every inch in between.

"Never go, you can't go," Efrosin cried, his voice ragged and wild.

Dmitri grabbed Efrosin close and held his shaking body, realizing he was shaking himself. He kissed him gently. "I'm here. Don't cry now, my Efrosin."

"But I must. I truly must."

Dmitri held Efrosin tight as the tears continued to flow, marveling at the number and intensity of them. It was as if Efrosin cried for all the wounds and pains of his life for which he'd never cried before. Dmitri stroked his back, murmuring, telling him not to fear—he'd live as long as Efrosin commanded him to live. This only set off fresh sobs.

Dmitri gritted his teeth as one of the knights bound Dmitri's foot tightly with cloth. The knight spoke to Geoffry. "His short-lived demise seems to have slowed the flow of blood. Still, he must have the wound attended to by the healer."

Geoffry nodded. "Of course." To Dmitri he said, "The sooner we go, the sooner you may be treated and my children's lives saved."

Dmitri frowned. "Your children?"

Efrosin's tears did not stop flowing as Geoffry explained their predicament, and Dmitri held Efrosin close before forcing himself to his feet, wincing at the terrible pain in his foot. "Of course, we must go immediately."

Two of the knights helped Efrosin to his feet, and since walking was a feat of gravity that Efrosin did not yet entirely grasp, Sir Carlisle aided him in his steps. The other knights helped Dmitri hobble to the horses, and when they reached them Efrosin clutched Dmitri's hand.

"Dmitri, will you be all right here alone while you await my return with a healer? Should I leave one of the knights with you?" Efrosin sniffled loudly.

Dmitri swiped his thumb across Efrosin's wet cheek. "There's no need to wait. It was just as I told you. Death released my bonds. I am free." He'd tell Efrosin about his fairy heritage when lives didn't hang in the balance.

"Truly?"

"Truly."

Efrosin face brightened, and then his expression turned determined. "Bring the horses," he ordered the knights. "We must leave quickly."

Geoffry bowed his head in gratitude. "Yes, thank you. Let us make haste."

"Dmitri and I shall ride together."

"He is weak. You shall ride with me, sire." Sir Carlisle led over his horse.

Efrosin snatched away the reins. "I think not." With a grunt, he attempted to heave himself into the saddle as the horse neighed.

"Not a stallion, sire," Geoffry said. "Please, you may take my horse. She's steady and polite, not meant for hard riding like a knight's steed."

Efrosin, to Dmitri's surprise, didn't argue, and took the few troubled steps, assisted by Sir Carlisle, to the horse Geoffry proffered. He again tried to haul himself onto the saddle.

Sir Carlisle said, "You must first learn to befriend gravity, sire."

"There is no time like the present," Efrosin said in an odd mix of new gravitas, pragmatism and his usual cheerful lack of sense.

Sir Carlisle helped Efrosin get his leg over the animal's broad back. "Careful. Not too far or you'll fall off the other side."

"This gravity everyone loves so well is rather useless," Efrosin grumbled, his still-wet lashes sparkling in the midday sun.

"Useless?" Dmitri asked, gritting his teeth as Sir Carlisle helped him settle behind Efrosin atop the mare. "My Efrosin, you are not floating away into the clouds. Given my wish to keep you safe, I find that rather useful indeed."

Off they rode, travelling in a single line through the dense forest. Dmitri kept his arms tight around Efrosin and gazed about avidly, paying no attention to the throbbing from his foot, so eager was he for a glimpse of new lands. Suddenly there was an odd clacking sound in the distance.

His pulse raced as the woods thinned and they approached the growing din. There before him, a road wound into the distance—a road with many carts rumbling and horses clopping. He swallowed hard, thinking of his many books and the faraway lands he'd only read about. Tears prickled his eyes.

"Dmitri?" Efrosin asked. He glanced over his shoulder. "Are you well?"

The boundaries of Dmitri's world became as limitless as the sky itself. "Oh Efrosin. What a grand adventure this shall be."

Dmitri bent and kissed Efrosin's parted lips. It tasted of clouds. Of freedom.

$$Epilogue$$

ALONG, LONG time ago, the sun set on a kingdom that was changed from the one it rose upon. For the Light Prince was light no more, and his beloved was unbound.

After shocking the prince's father with evidence not only of Efrosin's life but of his sudden onset of gravity, Efrosin and Dmitri were tended to by healers, and Geoffry's children set free with nary a hair on their wee heads harmed.

And once it was confirmed that, yes, the prince's weighted condition would not be reversed, and yes, his consort would survive the loss of his toe, Efrosin and Dmitri celebrated their love and freedom with weeks of joyous trysting in every private corner of the castle.

Once they had both learned to walk—for one was unaccustomed to bearing weight, and the other unaccustomed to a left foot that bore no big toe—they travelled together to distant lands, exploring the world Dmitri had previously only dreamt of seeing. As they journeyed, their affection for one another grew deep roots of love until they were inseparable—always where there was one, there was the other.

While they were afar, Ereshkigal the witch called a meeting with the aging king. "Come with me," she said, reaching out to Leo with her mossy fingers, grinning with her black teeth. "Your power is waning. But I can return you to full strength. Come, and you may have all you've ever desired. We have always belonged to each other."

Leo, lusting for more power than was rightfully his, followed her and abandoned his kingdom. Efrosin and Dmitri hastened back from their travels at the news, and the young prince depended greatly on the steady, generous heart of his lover to help him during the kingdom's time of need.

The prince sent his best knights to seek Ereshkigal's lair or any sign of his father, to no avail. The witch and king seemed to have vanished deep into the very earth. When many months had come and gone, his father was declared dead and the Light Prince was made king. Geoffry, who had loved and cared for the prince over many years, was appointed his closest advisor, and the new king ruled with fairness and grace.

Not long after their return and Efrosin's coronation, a wedding was celebrated unlike any the kingdom had ever seen. Both grooms dressed in resplendent white and silver, and upon the bank of the river they repeated their vows before God and the world—before diving in for a swim.

Which leaves but one story to tell of another joyous day when the sun set again on a world made new.

Once upon a time, there was a kingdom at the edge of what was and what could never be. At the center of this kingdom was a castle, and within this castle was a king. Inside this king was a terribly happy heart.

For on that day, the king and his prince stood hand-in-hand in the birthing chamber watching over the delivery of their child. Neither particularly cared if it was a girl or a boy, only that it be born healthy—and preferably free of magical entanglements.

The maid who had offered her services to be mother of the heir squirmed on the massive oak bed and cried out, her swollen, naked body sweating. Efrosin turned his head away, burying his face in Dmitri's neck, whispering, "Let me know when I may look again. Dear God, the poor woman. We must reward her well."

Nine moons before, their lovingly obtained spendings had been mixed in a vial, and a midwife had deposited the contents deep within the maid, close to the mouth of her eager womb. The child had taken the very first month, so sure was it of its desire to be brought into the world.

When a cry filled the air, Dmitri felt something stir in his chest, an already-love that took his breath away. Beside him, his husband's eyes gleamed with tears as he smiled, weighted with the heaviness of emotion and the enormity of responsibility.

The sun burst into the room as the shutters were thrown wide. Efrosin and Dmitri stood framed in the window of the high turret room, holding their naked child between them.

"Kneel to your future Queen!"

The infant's wails were soon drowned out by the cheers of the people rising high into the sky. Dmitri smiled wide, for only he and their child heard over the roar of the crowd below the laughter bubbling up from Efrosin's chest, echoing the joy in his own heart.

And they all lived happily ever after.

THE END

OMEGA MINE:
The Search for a Soulmate

Grumpy, oblivious bear shifter finally recognizes his sweet, destined mate!

Opposites attract! Shifter universe!

Short Novel Length

Can an Alpha find his dream Omega on reality TV?

Alpha Hank Morrow is a police officer and Alpha bear shifter who has never found the right Omega. Without the steadying influence of a bond with his Omega, Hank's powerful Alpha senses are beginning to overwhelm and endanger not only him, but his fellow police officers and the entire city of White Edge. The chief of police and the governor sign Hank up for a reality TV show to help unmatched Alphas find their dream Omega.

Omega Mine: Search for a Soulmate certainly isn't Hank's idea of a great plan, but he's not given a choice. Now he's off to a tropical island to meet over one hundred potential Omegas in a televised version of hell.

Or is it?

Evan Vaughn is an unmatched Omega. He and Hank have actually met once before at an Alpha-Omega mixer, but apparently he didn't make much of an impression at the time. Will that change on the set of *Omega Mine*? And can anything real come out of a reality TV dating show? Hank and Evan are about to find out...

The Bachelor meets **Alpha-Omega romance!**

This book is nearly 40,000 words of an oblivious bear shifter finally meeting his soul bonded match and a happy ending you'll love! Warning: There is no mfm in this book. There is no ménage in this book. There is no cheating in this book. There is an attraction to someone that is not the other MC but it does not come to fruition.

If you like Erotic Fantasy, check out Leta Blake's Omegaverse or shifter books!

SLOW HEAT

Omegaverse with knotting and heats!
Series starter! Kindle Unlimited!
Younger alpha, older omega!
Full Novel Length

"Holy hotness, YES, LETA BLAKE, you just gave me another reason to love you."
— Jordan, Alpha Book Club

"Wow—I loved this book! Couldn't put it down. Those who like their mm romance on the hot side will looove this one!"
— Eli Easton, author of Blame It On The Mistletoe and the Howl at the Moon series

"Slow Heat is a really rich and well developed book, one that kept me eagerly reading to the last page."
— Jay, Joyfully Jay Reviews

"I loved this book. Really LOVED it. The author once again proves her extraordinary versatility. This book is so much more than a love story. So multi-layered. So wonderful."

– Katerina, Don't Love Me, Jack Reviews

"[Alpha/Omega] isn't everybody's cuppa, I can't say this book will be for everyone, but I can say that Slow Heat is some of the best I've read yet."

– Lisa, The Novel Approach

A lustful young alpha meets his match in an older omega with a past.

Professor Vale Aman has crafted a good life for himself. An unbonded omega in his mid-thirties, he's long since given up hope that he'll meet a compatible alpha, let alone his destined mate. He's fulfilled by his career, his poetry, his cat, and his friends.

When Jason Sabel, a much younger alpha, imprints on Vale in a shocking and public way, longings are ignited that can't be ignored. Fighting their strong sexual urges, Jason and Vale must agree to contract with each other before they can consummate their passion.

But for Vale, being with Jason means giving up his independence and placing his future in the hands of an untested alpha—as well as facing the scars of his own tumultuous past. He isn't sure it's worth it. But Jason isn't giving up his destined mate without a fight.

This is a stand-alone gay romance novel, 118,000 words, with a strong HFN ending, as well as a well-crafted, non-shifter omegaverse, with alphas, betas, omegas, male pregnancy, heat, and knotting. Content warning for pregnancy loss and aftermath.

HEAT FOR SALE

Omegaverse with knotting, heat, and pregnancy!

Erotic with interesting world-building!

Older alpha, younger omega!

"This book is as hot as the proverbial fires of hell."

– Mirrigold Reviews.

Heat can be sold but love is earned.

In a world where omegas sell their heats for profit, Adrien is a university student in need of funding. With no family to fall back on, he reluctantly allows the university's matcher to offer his virgin heat for auction online. Anxious, but aware this is the reality of life for all omegas, Adrien hopes whoever wins his heat will be kind.

Heath—a wealthy, older alpha—is rocked by the young man's resemblance to his dead lover, Nathan. When Heath discovers Adrien is Nathan's lost son from his first heat years before they met, he becomes obsessed with the idea of reclaiming a piece of Nathan.

Heath buys Adrien's heat with only one motivation: to impregnate Adrien, claim the child, and move on. But their undeniable passion shocks him. Adrien doesn't know what to make of the handsome, mysterious stranger he's pledged his body to, but he's soon swept away in the heat of the moment and surrenders to Heath entirely.

Once Adrien is pregnant, Heath secrets him away to his immense and secluded home. As the birth draws near, Heath grows to love Adrien for the man he is, not just for his connection to Nathan. Unaware of Heath's past with his omega parent and coming to depend on him, heart and soul, Adrien begins to fall as well.

But as their love blossoms, Nathan's shadow looms. Can Heath keep his new love and the child they've made together once Adrien discovers his secrets?

Heat for Sale is a stand-alone m/m erotic romance by Leta Blake. Infused with a du Maurier Rebecca-style secret, it features a well-realized omegaverse, an age-gap, dominance and submission, heats, knotting, and scorching hot scenes.

New Adult

Punching the V-Card

'90s Coming of Age Series
Pictures of You
You Are Not Me
Only You

Winter Holidays

North's Pole

The Mr. Christmas Series
Mr. Frosty Pants
Mr. Naughty List
Mr. Jingle Bells

A Boy for All Seasons
My December Daddy

Fantasy

Any Given Lifetime

Reimagined Fairy Tales

Flight
Levity

Paranormal & Shifters

Angel Undone
Omega Mine

Horror

Raise Up Heart

Omegaverse

Heat of Love Series
White Heat
Slow Heat

Alpha Heat
Slow Birth
Bitter Heat

For Sale Series
Heat for Sale
Bully for Sale

Audiobooks
letablake.com/audiobooks

Discover more about the author online

Leta Blake
letablake.com

Gay Romance Newsletter

Leta's newsletter will keep you up to date on her latest releases, sales and deals, future writing plans, and more from the world of M/M romance. Join Leta's mailing list today.

Leta Blake on Patreon

Become part of Leta Blake's Patreon community to support her indie publishing expenses and to access exclusive content, deleted scenes, extras, and interviews.

Author of the bestselling book *Smoky Mountain Dreams* and fan favorites like *Training Season*, *Will & Patrick Wake Up Married*, and *Slow Heat*, Leta Blake has been captivating M/M Romance readers for over a decade. Whether writing contemporary romance or fantasy, she puts her psychology background to use creating complex characters and love stories that feel real. At home in the Southern U.S., Leta works hard at achieving balance between her writing and her family life.